O'BRIEN, LIPSCHITZ, AND PARTNERS

A Satire

Written and Illustrated by:

JOHN NIEMAN

Inquiries and Book Orders should be addressed to:

Great Writers Media
Email: info@greatwritersmedia.com
Phone: 877-600-5469

ISBN: 978-1-959493-50-1 (sc)
ISBN: 978-1-959493-51-8 (ebk)

CONTENTS

For all my creative, courageous, and outrageous friends who brightened my years in the advertising business.

PREFACE

Before I became an artist and an author, I spent thirty years in the advertising business. For the most part, it was loads of fun. I remember coming up with dozens of ideas, sometimes in a week. As a former actor, I loved pitching new business. I was proud to get many spots in the Super Bowl. As a worldwide creative director, I was particularly fond of the global travel (180 days a year). As I look back on my résumé, I was fortunate to work at many of the top ten advertising agencies and create work for Coca-Cola, Anheuser-Busch, Hallmark, Burger King, Mars, Qantas, Cadillac, Lincoln-Mercury, P&G, and dozens of other adventurous brands.

This particular business is in a perpetual state of change. It always has been. An agency that is "hot" may be old news in a few years. An old-fart agency may gain a renaissance with a new creative director. And of course, social media has changed things dramatically.

One thing I have particularly noticed in recent years is that "straight, feature-benefit" advertising doesn't gain much attention, unless the client has a multimillion-dollar budget. Humor works. Outrageous gains headlines. Anything unexpected earns a certain amount of respect.

That new inclination is the gist of this book.

The other factor is the people who work at an ad agency. Some are goofy. Some are reticent. Some are straight. Some are gay. Most are liberal. Some are archconservatives. The combination of these types creates a fabric that I always found interesting.

It's an exciting environment. As you turn the pages, I hope you will find it to be one.

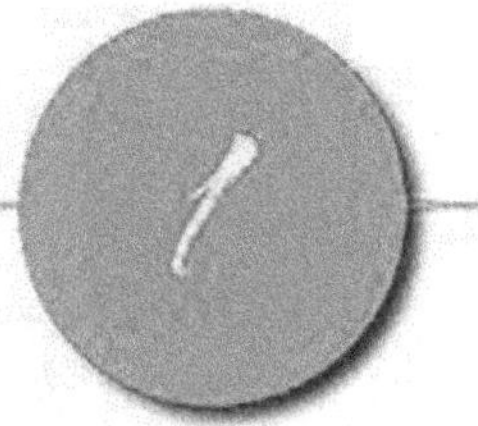

Out of the Blue

According to most pundits on Madison Avenue, Ogilvy & Mather was a slam dunk to win this account. For starters, they were on a hot streak, having won Merrill Lynch, FedEx, Unicef, AT&T, and Johnson & Johnson baby powder over the past twelve months.

Admittedly, these were not the most creatively challenging accounts in advertising industry. However, that was not O&M's stock and trade. They were known as a solid, business-oriented agency, and a very successful one at that—both in the USA and internationally.

Consequently, it was widely assumed that the Serta mattress company in the Midwest would be a perfect fit with the agency.

The key point person on this pitch was a woman named Shelly Lipschitz, who had five years' experience as an account manager and two years at the helm as new business director. She was smart and had a savvy, intuitive instinct of client needs, and she was good on her feet in a presentation. To her board of directors, she declared, "If there is ever an ideal client for Ogilvy, it is Serta. After all, nobody knows feature-benefit advertising better than us. Besides, we are pitching against the minor leagues. I guarantee we will win this account!"

And yet, her antennae told her that this was not a straight-ahead, a "dot the i's and cross all the t's" kind of pitch. The client had hinted more than once that they would like to be surprised. She told her creative staff in charge of creating a prototype campaign, "Don't take this one for granted. I've got a hunch they may want something slightly out of the box."

The creative staff toiled for a week or so and came up with "S-E-R-T-A— how you spell comfort." The commercial featured vignettes of men, women, and kids against sleepy music. The head copywriter on the pitch bragged about the spelling of the client's brand. "That will stick in people's brain. They might even repeat it going down the street or going into a mattress store."

"Really," Shelly asked skeptically. "Did you have another campaign or two that was a close second?"

"The consensus of the group was that this one was the clear winner. People need a good night's sleep to compete in today's world," the creative guy said. "Maybe you should put that in the ad," Shelly advised. "That sounds meaningful."

As in most big advertising agencies, the creative people do not like to take advice from account people. However, it did sound like a good idea. Reluctantly, the creative guy said he could probably add a short sentence in the spot to indicate that a good night's sleep in comfort can add to success in the next day.

"Yes," Shelly appreciated the concession. "But don't spell out success, S- U-C-C-E-S-S," she added with private sarcasm.

"No, no, no. That would be too much. The only thing we spell out would be S-E-R-T-A."

"Good," Shelly said with some irony. "Go to it."

After the group left her office, Shelly sat at her desk, shaking her head at the state of the advertising business. It was more fun seven years ago, before she started guaranteeing to the board of directors that they would definitely win this next new business pitch.

Rather than dwell on it, she began to create "the deck"—basically a reasoned dossier about why Ogilvy & Mather would be the perfect partner for Serta. It began with the client's business. It outlined their issues and opportunities in today's world. It then chronicled O&M's track record with similar clients, along with samples of their more famous ads. At least the last half of the document addressed the agency's particular approach for Serta. As a sop to the creative staff, she did make some hay about spelling out the Serta name. She also stressed the importance of a good night's sleep in comfort— how it makes a difference in the next morning's acuity, balance, creativity, and spontaneity.

She actually researched this topic online and found it to be quite true. According to the AMA, a good night's sleep (with good REM dreams) "makes an amazing quantifiable difference in productivity the following morning."

She sent that link to the creative guy in charge of the pitch. He sent back a smug email. "We've already included a sentence to that effect. Please stress the S-E-R-T-A spelling of the brand."

With a sigh, Shelly completed the document, which was seventy-four pages long. She then tried to assess her competition on this pitch. There were two midsize ad agencies from Chicago, which might give them a geographical advantage for the Illinois client. However, they did not seem to have stellar reels or great raves from their clients. There was a rather successful midsize agency in NYC called Tatham-Laird & Kudner. Not bad, but not a great track record on new business pitches. And then there was an oddball entry—an upstart agency called O'Brien, O'Brien. It had all of three employees. One of them was Ryan O'Brien, a senior account guy who spent decades at Y&R, where he dealt with many big-ticket clients and continued with many contacts in his senior years. Perhaps he had a personal connection with the Serta client. Otherwise, why would they be in this pitch? The other principal? His son, Jack O'Brien, a haywire creative guy who had written some nutsy campaigns for his clients at several boutique agencies. He was definitely out of the box. And the third employee was a woman named Naomi, who was the receptionist for the shop and a cheerful presence at the agency.

The notion that this oddball agency was even included made no sense to Shelly. It was an option out of nowhere, completely out of the blue.

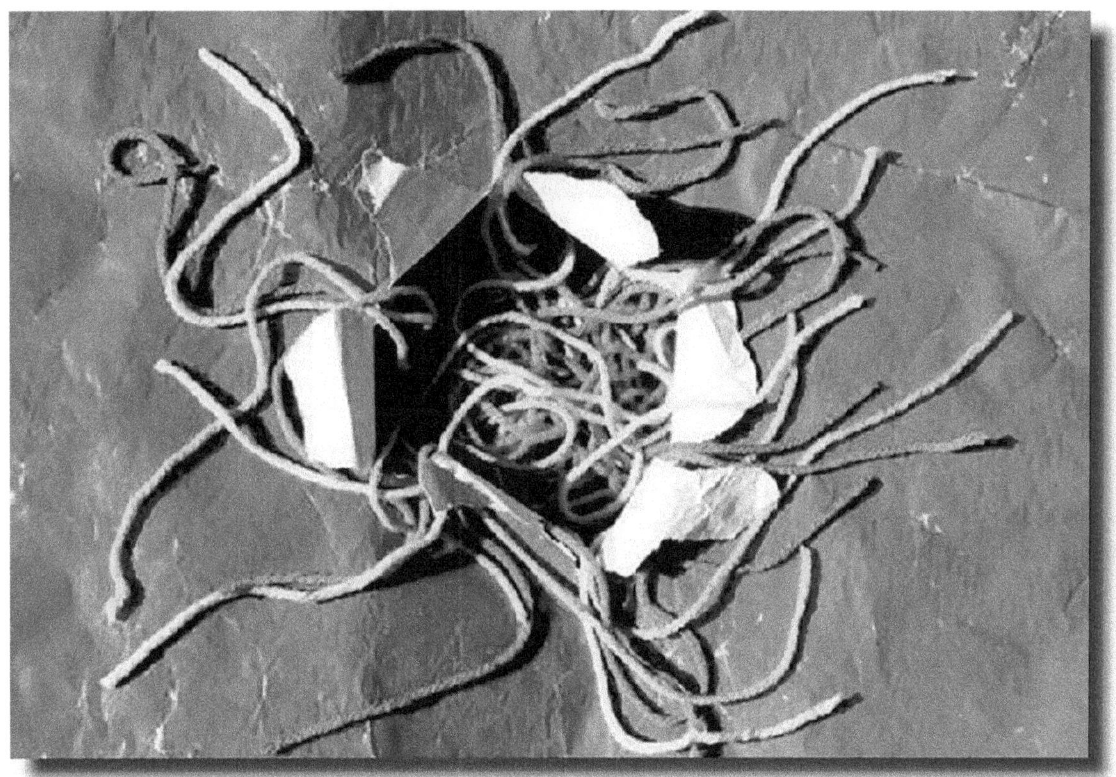

Shelly felt capable of defeating every other agency in this pitch, but the upstart agency gave her pause. "What do they have to lose?" she asked herself. They could present the most outrageous campaign and gain points just because they were different.

On the internet, there was little to be learned about young Jack O'Brien. In his early years, he was the copywriter at several New York agencies, where he did mediocre work for the US Postal Service ("We deliver, we deliver") and Yuban Coffee ("Ooh, it's rich"). And then he turned to more aggressive, more outrageous work. It included work for Art Fair NYC, Gotham Comedy Club, and the *National Enquirer*.

As a defense, she prepared a slide-show presentation on the value of a good night's sleep in comfort. It highlighted many of the findings of the American Medical Association. It was intelligent. It was cogent. But it did not match the creative presentation, which wished to stress the spelling of S-E-R-T-A.

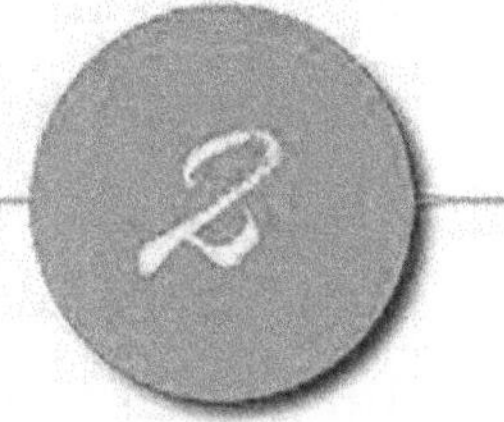

On the Other Hand

Thanks to his father's contacts with certain Serta clients, Jack O'Brien had been invited to share his thoughts on Serta.

He had crafted a safe campaign called 800 Springs and scrapped it after having too many Budweisers. He pitched a campaign the next day called Sleep Sexy, which featured a porn star, Stormy Daniels, who would later become famous for her $130,000 payout from President Donald Trump's lawyer.

He had seen her show at FlashDancers Gentlemen's Club on West Fifty- Second and asked her if she would be interested in being in a commercial.

"Sure!" was her response, with a kiss on the lips. "Do you have a head shot?" O'Brien asked.

In the actual new business pitch, the creative director asked the Serta client, "What are the two major functions of a mattress?"

Somewhat flummoxed by the question, Jack O'Brien jumped in and answered for the business leaders in their Brooks Brothers suits. "Number 1 is comfort and a good night's sleep. But you guys are the acknowledged leader in that category. No one even comes close. So there's no news value in that claim. It's just telling people what they already know."

O'Brien looked at the conference table and could see the Serta executives nodding in agreement.

"I say we be bold. Let's be memorable. Let's capture the hidden, unspoken value of a good mattress. Do I need to spell it out for you?" he asked, and he asked for a clean sheet of paper. He then wrote the letters S-E-X.

The rather straight MBAs from Serta blushed but did smile at the ingenuity of the presentation. When O'Brien passed out the head shot of Stormy Daniels, it was something of a slam dunk. Especially since the creative director revisited her striptease act and persuaded her at twenty dollars per shot to have autographed pictures of the porn star for each of the Serta decision makers. It basically said, "Dear Ed, sleep sexy with Serta, Your friend, Stormy."

In the actual pitch, Jack O'Brien did deliver a rather straight script for the porn star and as justification for the mattress company to run the ad. The copy extolled the 800 Springs ("Up and down, up and down, eight hundred ways," according to alluring Stormy Daniels).

After all the other agencies had presented their "Sleep in comfort" campaigns to Serta, the executives finally decided to give this unexpected approach a try and reward the business to Jack O'Brien.

Ironically, he had pitched and won the account in a shoot-out against Shelly Lipschitz, who had a presented a seventy-four-page deck to the Serta executives about the "S-E-R-T-A spells comfort" campaign.

It took the decision-making committee about forty-five minutes to award the business to the brash presentation of Jack O'Brien. That night, Jack and his newfound Serta executives went to FlashDancers Gentlemen's Club on West Fifty-Second and gained lipstick kiss impressions on each of their photos from Stormy Daniels.

The very next week, the decision was the talk of *Ad Age* and *Adweek*, and it helped forge a new adventurous thrust in the advertising business and a new alliance between the outrageous Jack O'Brien and the most brilliant account person on Madison Avenue, Shelly Lipschitz.

The New, Weird Agency

Shelly Lipschitz, the reigning queen of Madison Avenue new business, could not believe she actually had been beaten in the chase for a coveted new client. In the past twelve months, she had won virtually every pitch. And she had guaranteed the win for O&M.

Lesson: Don't guarantee in a changing market. In her thirty-minute conversation with the Serta executives, she learned that even the rather straight world of household products, her pitch was seen as too straight, too solid, too intellectual. Ultimately, too boring.

"So what did you settle on?" she asked with some trepidation.

"Sleep sexy with Serta," she heard from George F. Winston, who was the chief marketing officer of the mattress company.

After a three-second pause, Shelly involuntarily responded, "Are you fucking kidding me?"

After another three-second pause, George remembered her agency's recommended theme line. "What? You think, 'S-E-R-T-A spells comfort' will move more mattresses?" He did not wait for a response. "Shelly, the world is changing. We cannot be so safe in the years ahead. I know, I know … your proposal was the smartest but not the most exciting in these days. We decided to go outside the box and maybe take a chance."

Atypically for Ms. Lipschitz, there was at least a ten-second pause. It sunk in. Smart was not enough. In the days ahead, courageous could count. More to the point, semicrazy could count.

After an hour of letting this disappointing verdict sink in, Shelly actually called the schmuck she had never called in her life—a Mr. Jack O'Brien, the guy who had clearly and winningly outpointed her in her last new business pitch.

"Hello? I would like to speak with the winner!" Shelly aggressively admitted.

"Sleep sexy … with Serta!" Jack O'Brien gleefully responded without even knowing who was calling, despite a half dozen communiqués about the audacious new campaign.

"Is this Mr. Jack O'Brien?" she responded.

"The one and only," he said. "Wait. Let me get out of my sexy Serta mattress here and try to address whatever is on your mind. Ooh. Ooh. Ooh. I'll be back in a minute, hon." He seemed to be talking with a perhaps imaginary love interest.

"I guess congratulations are in order," Shelly said and introduced herself. "It's boffo news," Jack answered. "I think my ad career has absolutely gone into orbit."

Looking at the morning newspapers, Shelly Lipchitz had to silently admit that his prediction was perhaps true. At her desk, she had reviewed the advertising news before this call.

"Audacious new campaign wins new Serta account" was reported in the *New York Times* ad column. "Omigod, sex actually sells. Is anyone surprised?" was the headline in the *New York Post*.

"Would you like to have a lunch?"

"I don't generally think beyond the next twenty-four hours," Jack answered. "I heard about your 'Sleep in comfort' campaign."

"And?"

After a few seconds, Jack again responded, "Sorry, I fell asleep hearing your boring theme line."

To both individual's surprise, lunch was not boring. As a matter of fact, they had a few laughs and agreement that advertising should be more exciting and unexpected. After a few more lunches, they actually decided to join forces and create a new model for a small New York agency—one that was smart and wildly creative.

In November, *Adweek* dubbed them as the most courageous, outrageous, unpredictable advertising agency in Manhattan. "Sometimes, they come up with irreverent campaigns. Many advertising veterans predict it will never work. However, given the national desire to break from the status quo and an undeniable embrace of the politically incorrect, they have become the talk of the town. The question is, Can it possibly last? Is this a phase? Will they burn out? One wonders, but for the time being, they are hot as a comet."

As for a locale, the duo chose the Chelsea neighborhood district of NYC— an area replete with famous art galleries, which the owners decided would inevitably give the agency some allure and some stall time if they were inevitably late for a meeting.

To prepare for that eventuality, Jack O'Brien had visited some of the local galleries such as Agora and Viridian galleries to pay homage to the area, help decorate the space of West

Twenty-Eighth, and lay the pipe for good recommendations for wealthy clients who might visit their exhibitions in the days ahead.

Fortunately for O'Brien, Lipschitz, and Partners, they did not need much stall time. The next twelve months were filled with new business activity.

Herbert Hooter

The agency's big breakthrough campaign happened in the next few months. On a drive home on the West Side Highway, Ryan O'Brien saw the big glaring sign for Hooters—exit right. He took the turn, and in the process of his enjoyable evening, he contacted the bartender and promised that his new agency (actually his son's new agency) could make them even more famous.

"I'd like to leave my business card for you," Ryan said to the bartender. "Also, do you have a manager here? Is there a chance I could meet him and give him my contact information?"

"Sure. Jimmy!" the bartender called out to a man in his late thirties, who seemed to be central casting for a young, successful boss. When the executive came to the bar, the bartender introduced Ryan O'Brien and looked at his business card. "Wow, he is the chairman emeritus of a big hotshot New York ad agency."

"Jimmy Randall," the executive said. He extended his hand for a welcoming hello.

"Nice place," Ryan said. "Looks like people have fun here," the older man said and followed one of the buxom waitresses with his eyes.

"The food's good too, but I'm not sure we get enough credit for our recipes. You got experience selling the quality of the food?"

"Tons," Ryan answered. "Kraft, Green Giant, TGI Fridays, Sardi's. Of course, that's just my ancient history. My son and his partner, Shelly, have more recent experience. And their age range is a little more in line with the clientele. They're good. You would not be disappointed."

"You're pretty persuasive," Jimmy admitted.

"Not as persuasive as my creative son and his account sidekick. If you give me your card, I'll have them call you and set up a hello."

"Sounds like a plan." Jimmy smiled. "I'm going to expect a call from you or your underlings, and we'll try to build our reputation for recipes. It was nice to meet you, Ryan O'Brien."

"And nice to meet you, Jimmy Randall," the patriarch of the new agency said with as much full sincerity as he could muster after so many jaded decades in the ad biz.

The next morning, Ryan met with his son, Shelly Lipschitz, and Martin Parsons, the planner.

"Hooters, the bimbo joint," Shelly reacted with horror.

"They would like to be taken more seriously for their food," Ryan submitted.

"Boob food," Shelly lashed out.

After a take, Ryan executed his learned account-man BS, almost Jesuitical logic. "First of all, it's not a striptease joint. It's just twentysomething women in T-shirts. All they want is to be taken more seriously for the food."

"Aw, come on. Get real," she objected.

"OK, let me ask you this, Shelly," Ryan pushed a new argument. "What if we were given the opportunity to pitch Club Med singles clubs, where all the women parade topless and everybody shacks up every night? Would that be OK with you?"

Perplexed by the trap, Shelly had to think about it. "I think that would be OK. It's consensual."

"And this isn't?" Ryan objected.

After a few seconds of thinking about the dilemma, Martin Parsons saved the silence. "I for one would very much like to see the place. I hear the environment is quite beautiful. Hee, hee, hee."

"I'll go with you," Jack O'Brien volunteered. "Nothing ventured, nothing gained."

"Omigod, should we rename our place the nightmare agency?" Shelly asked.

"Dad, do you want to join us?"

"No, I already met Jimmy, and I'm too old for the place. But I think you should bring a woman as well to make it feel like a legit meeting. If not Shelly, then maybe Tess could go with you."

In their initial meeting at the Hooters bar, Jimmy was all smiles, especially since O'Brien, Lipschitz, and Partners had sent them a full thirty-two-page dossier of the new agency's capabilities and their proposal to at least put more emphasis on the food. In private conversations with the chairman emeritus, Jimmy did admit he didn't want to totally disqualify the other more physical attractions of the place.

In their initial interview, Jack O'Brien, Tess D'Emelia, and Martin Parsons requested a private table at 7:00 p.m. to taste the offerings. In addition, they had requested Jimmy to meet with them for at least a half hour to clarify the mission.

"Tess, are you put off by this display at all?" Jimmy asked the attractive art director.

"Not at all. This is just business."

Jack O'Brien could barely resist reaching over the table to kiss her on the lips for her politically correct response.

"I personally love this place," Martin avowed. "Hey, these women are beautiful," he said, looking to the right and left as all the waitresses balanced heavy trays.

"We're here to talk about the food," Jack O'Brien, in an atypical stance of maturity, stated. "Was there a founding father for this chain? Someone like Colonel Sanders? Orville Redenbacher? Ray Kroc? Chef Boyardee?"

"I don't think so. It did not get its start on cuisine."

"I can see that," Martin observed, looking at a Latina woman carrying food to the table.

After a rather uncomfortable pause, Tess volunteered a creative thought. "There's no reason we couldn't *invent* a founder."

"I like the way you think," Jack announced to his creative partner.

"Order anything you want. Sample the menu," Jimmy volunteered with a smile. "My treat. And when you're ready with an award-winning campaign, let's set up a meeting." The manager bowed to the crowd and made a graceful exit.

The members of the agency ordered some chicken wings, curly fries, an onion ring tower, a Caesar salad, and a round of caramel fudge cheesecake.

"Whadya think?" Jack asked his art director.

"Well, it's the farthest thing from health food, but it's pretty tasty," Tess diplomatically answered.

"I think it's delicious," Martin, the strategic planner, joined in. "And have you noticed the waitresses? They're beautiful!"

Even Jack O'Brien had to shake his head at the obviousness of his cohort's reaction. On the way out, he did stop and thank Jimmy for the gratis dinner and promised to be back to him soon with a groundbreaking advertising campaign.

"I look forward to it," Jimmy answered and waved adios to the small entourage from O'Brien, Lipschitz, and Partners.

It took them only three weeks to come up with an eye-popping campaign. On the basis of Tess's suggestion that they create their own food guru for Hooters, they invented a character called Herbert Hooter. According to the invented legend, he had always wanted to create tantalizing tastes for the mouth and was the progenitor of the Hooters food legend.

Who could play the role? They did not want a young stud—too predictable, given the aura of the place. Instead, they went for off-center fire and negotiated a deal with the comedian Jim Carey. Jack O'Brien liked the fact that he seemed to have a forever glint in his eye, a naughty mind, and a mock-serious tone about cuisine. In the early days of their negotiations,

Carey was not too amenable to being the spokesman for Hooters. However, as he saw the scripts, he did sign up and agree to shoot a few prototypical commercials.

The first one only featured his voice-over. It introduced a young twelve- year-old in the streets of Texas as he longed to satiate his appetites.

As the commercial begins, we see a kid at a Texas crossroads, a la *North by Northwest,* and a remembrance of the early years. Within a few seconds, a few women in tight Hooters T-shirts bring in some plates of food, which seems to satisfy the young man. The kid can barely keep his eyes off the sexy women and then enjoys a french fry. Against this visual back-drop, we hear Jim Carey's voice.

Carey: Even at an early age, I knew I had appetites. Hello there. (*He is responding to a Hooters girl serving some french fries.*) I always knew that when I sat down to eat, I would like to smile. (*Another buxom woman brings in some sliders.*) So I created Hooters, and I have been satisfied ever since. Come. Experience. Discover. Va-va-va food!

The commercial only ran for a few weeks but created quite a sensation since it featured a teenager obviously attracted to a Playboy Bunny.

The payoff spot actually featured Jim Carey on camera. It was basically a one-scene commercial. It featured Jim being served several entrées by beautiful, busty, T-shirted women.

This was the script:

"I'm Herbert Hooter. I created this menu. Chicken breast sticks, and speaking of breasts … (*He observes the large boobs of the woman who just placed the plate in front of him.*)

"Naked wings. We can only wish! (*He accepts a plate by another buxom server.*)

"Lots-a-tots! Potatoes. Bacon. Cheese. Sour cream. Green onions. How bad can we be in one day? (*Jim looks at the waitress who serves this sinful dish and follows her out of frame with his eyes.*)

"Desserts? (*He views another woman who crosses in front of the camera.*) Need I say more?

"Take it from me, Herbert Hooter. Hooters in your neighborhood."

As Jim Carey sees women walking to his left and right and everywhere in between, he sums up his message: "Hooters. Va-va-va-food!"

When the campaign was presented to Jimmy Randall at Hooters, the manager stood up and applauded. Even Shelly Lipschitz attended the presentation and was all smiles.

"Brilliant," Jimmy gushed. "I love the fact that you combined our new emphasis on food quality with our existing environmental equities. And the line, 'Va-va-va food'? Excellent! We're gonna run the shit out of these commercials!"

Indeed, they did. The commercials became ubiquitous on sports programming and late-night shows. Within weeks, people would come into the restaurant and greet the receptionist with the phrase "Va-va-va food."

The commercial even won a coveted gold lion at the Cannes Film Festival for commercials. When it was played, the international audience went wild with applause. When Jack O'Brien and Shelly Lipschitz walked onto the stage to accept the award, the creative director held the trophy over his head and simply responded, "Va-va-va-thanks."

In the auditorium, Jack's father, Ryan, sat there with a smile on his face.

He fully believed he had made an impact on the agency's fortunes and earned his expense account at least for the next few years.

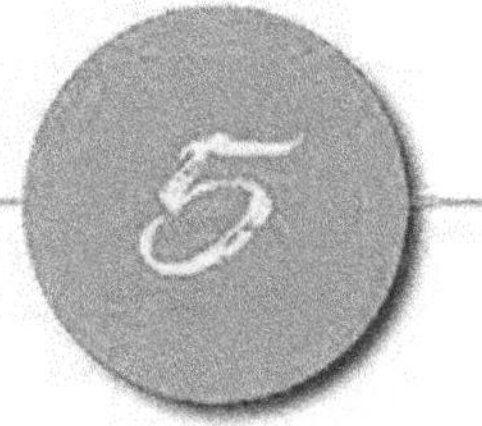

Be the Only One in Your City to Drive One

There are many wildly popular cars sold in the United States—Ford, Honda, Nissan, Toyota, Jeep SUVs, Chevy trucks. You see them on every highway.

The Fiat 500L is not one of these magnificent successes. As a matter of fact, it is truly one of the least popular cars sold in America. Part of its problem is that it doesn't easily fit into an easy category. It's not really a small, easy-to-maneuver economy car, and it's slightly too petite for an SUV. Worse yet, it has the most complaints of any car sold in the States. According to J. D. Powers, there are more than two hundred problems or customer complaints per one hundred Fiats that are sold. Consequently, these cars sit on dealer lots longer than most other alternatives—approximately 140 days, gathering dust while waiting for a willing customer.

Perhaps that's why this Italian division of Chrysler knocked on the door of O'Brien, Lipschitz, and Partners.

A rather elegant Fiat executive named Emilio Giannino introduced himself to Shelly Lipschitz while flourishing his silk scarf around his neck and giving her a kiss on the hand. "Buongiorno," he announced with a bow and launched on his charm offensive.

After some inevitable chitchat about the wonders of Manhattan and comparisons to Torino, Italy, Emilio presented his business card and came to the point. "We make one of the most wonderful vehicles in the world. It's easy-to-maneuver and so very stylish … in an economical way. But here in the US, people do not feel special driving the Fiat 500L. Imagine that?"

"And what's been your experience with your regular Chrysler/Fiat agencies?" Shelly pushed back, accustomed to hearing much international bullshit from her prior clients in multinational agencies.

"They are afraid to be bold," Emilio responded almost as if he had rehearsed. "The brand needs something brash—aggressive, even sexy. Why not? After all, we are Italian," he said with a smile and a wink.

"Budget?" she asked pointedly.

"Oooh," the Italian executive objected. "I hate the fact that in our first meeting, it is such a financial deal."

Shelly riposted, "I just want to know if we are in the same ballpark. We have become very popular these days, and I need to know if this is worth our energy."

Obviously prepared for the rebuttal, Emilio announced matter-of-factly, "We might entertain a five-million-dollar budget."

"We might be able to do business," Shelly responded. "And I think it might be a truly exciting relationship. Given our talents and insights, I am confident we can make a difference. Just so you know, our most senior art director is an Italian woman called Tess D'Emelia, who might have a special affinity for this brand."

"That's so great. I trust that I might hear from you in the next few weeks." The Italian gentleman bowed and smiled.

"Nobody wants to buy the damn car," Shelly explained to Jack, Tess, and Martin in their briefing a few days later, after she had done some homework and gathered some catalogues on the least popular car in America.

"It's an ugly motherfucker," Jack immediately reacted upon looking at the pictures of the vehicles.

"I'm sure we could make it look semiattractive," Tess offered, imagining some low-angle photography and Italian imagery.

Shelly tried to direct the focus of the discussion. She held up her hand and addressed the small group. "It's not so much about the appearance of the car or the lack of sales. According to the client, it's a user-imagery problem. According to Mr. Giannino, no one is proud to drive this vehicle. And I think that hurts his feelings."

"As a proud Italian American, I can understand that emotion," Tess admitted.

"Who drives it?" Martin, the strategic planner, asked.

"Dumb shits," Shelly answered. "Geeks, cheapskates. Admittedly, it is the least popular automobile brand in America."

"Whoa, I like that," Jack avowed. "It could be sort of reverse snobbery thing. Hey, why drive a Bentley or a Jaguar or Rolls when you can drive a Fiat?"

The room laughed, and then the thought sunk in. "That's not so stupid," Martin interjected. "Maybe we make the rare driver of this loser car feel like a special, one-of-a-kind, unique person—so unlike the herd, so unlike everyone who mindlessly follows the pack."

The conference room stopped laughing. "I like that," Jack finally said.

"Could we get some interviews of the few dumb shits who actually bought this car?" Tess asked.

"I'm sure we could," Shelly answered.

"All we have to do is make that one idiot seem like the most discriminating buyer in all of New York City," Martin offered. Almost like a sports huddle, everyone in the room high-fived each other at this stroke of brilliance.

After interviewing three buyers in the New York metro area, the agency settled on a Mr. Gavino Biasi, who had owned one for the past three years in Flatbush, Queens. He was a FedEx delivery guy who primarily drove his truck to unload packages but did need the small economical car on the evenings and weekends. An added plus was this: he had an Italian accent and some genuine affection for the brand. Just as a bonus, his Fiat was a bright- red color and in relatively good shape.

After several interviews by Jack, Martin and few ciaos by Tessa, the script was set. Basically, it would be a one-day shoot with testimonial copy from the Fiat owner.

The thirty-second commercial begins in the parking lot of an A&P shopping lot. Our hero is exiting his Fiat and is greeted by a beautiful Italian American woman.

"Everywhere I go, people ask me, 'What kind of special car is that you are driving?'"

"Wow," the attractive woman says with a thumbs-up.

"Sometimes, I just say, 'It's my secret,'" the man says, and he chuckles. The star of the commercial pulls into a gas station.

"Hey, you don't come in here very often," the attendant says.

"Well, that's cause this amazing vehicle doesn't require much gas," the owner responds and smiles.

The driver pulls into a parallel parking spot. A newspaper reporter comes up to him. "Are you famous?" he asks. "Should I know you?"

"Have you ever been to the Oscars?" our hero asks with some ironic sarcasm.

"Were you the best actor of the year last year?" the reporter asks. "No autographs, please," our hero says and dashes off.

Cut. In the next scene, a cop on the highway is stopping our star. Gavino asks, "Was I speeding?"

Cop answers, "No, I just wanted to know what kind of car that was. Very unique. I see everything on this thruway. But this is special."

The commercial ends with a series of comments from people who observe the driver and the Fiat.

"Do I know you?" one teenager says to the driver in a parking spot.

"Wow, who are you?" a scantily clad woman with a boa says to our hero as he exits his vehicle.

"Should I know you by your car?" a woman asks the man innocently, and in a rather overacted moment, our hero shrugs, with an implication of "Who doesn't know this car?"

The voice-over announcer sums up the message: "His name is the one and only Gavino Biasi. His car is the one and only Fiat 500L."

After a pause, the announcer speaks with emphasis. "Gavino. Fiat. Be the only one in your city to drive one."

When the commercial was played in the screening room for the Italian client, he actually took out a handkerchief to wipe away his tears. After composing himself, he said, "That is everything that I could ever hope this commercial could be. Yes, yes, yes, you feel special driving this car. *Gracie. Gracie. Gracie.*"

He then left the agency and joined his driver, in a Lincoln Continental, who drove him back to his plush office in midtown Manhattan.

The Truth ... with a Twist

On the heels of this international accolade, *Ad Age* decided to run a feature story on O'Brien, Lipschitz, and Partners. According to the publication, "the agency has become the weirdest, most outrageous and creative agency in the business."

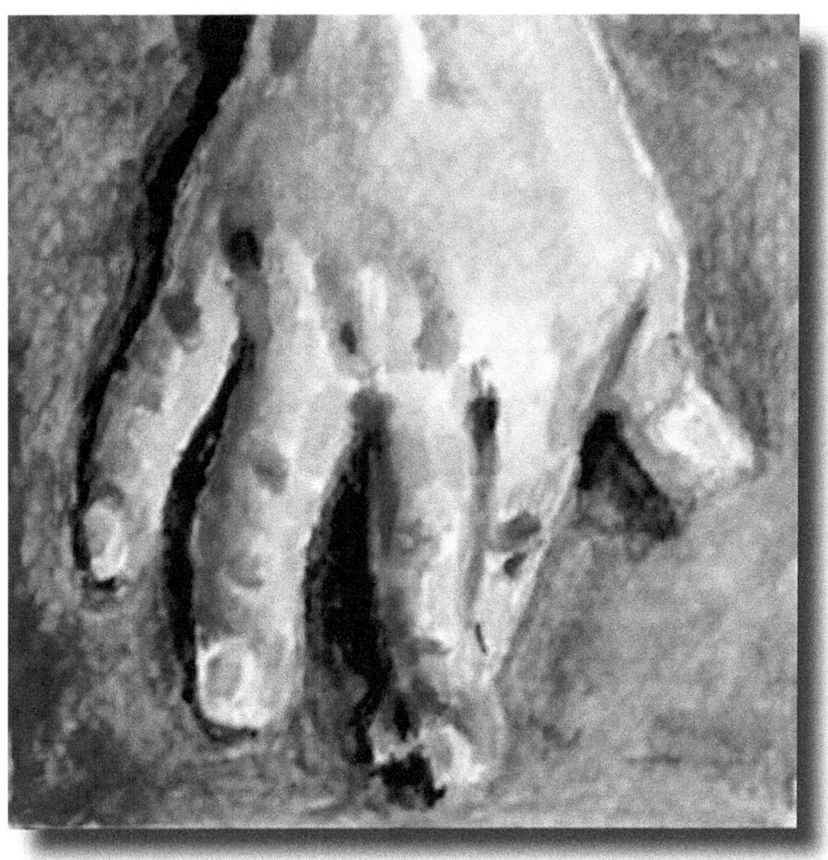

The profile would feature their reel of commercials and include an interview with Jack O'Brien and Shelly Lipschitz, where they would be asked to give their viewpoint on the state of the industry and their personal philosophy of advertising.

The reporter, a young man named Michael Ortiz, arrived on time with his publication's photographer, a woman named Lara Carlyle. They were escorted by the receptionist to the conference room and were offered coffee or soda.

Within minutes, Shelly and Jack entered the room. Jack was carrying the Cannes gold lion and placed it in the center of the conference room, perhaps to subconsciously focus the interview of their award-winning work.

After introductions, Michael Ortiz asked the traditional interviewer's question: "Do you mind if I record this conversation so I can honestly listen to your questions without taking notes?"

"Fine, we are used to it," Shelly answered.

The reporter then put a small electronic gizmo on the conference table and hit the record button. He then introduced his photographer and explained that she would be shooting candid shots, with their permission, of course.

"Shoot away." Jack smiled back.

After a few moments of looking in his notebook, Michael began the interview with an easy question, "What do you think of the current state of advertising?"

Jack had been asked this question a few times from prospective clients and his staff. Even though it was a rehearsed answer, the creative director did his best to deliver the answer as if he had just heard the question for the first time and was constructing an impromptu response.

"I think the quality of advertising is at a low point," Jack said. "So much of it is bullshit," he added. Looking at the recording device, O'Brien then held up his hands in an apparent apology. "Omigod, I hate to use profanity in an interview such as this. Perhaps you can just change that to BS. Everyone will know what that means without saying the actual *bullshit* word."

Truth be told, Jack loved disarming reporters early in his interviews. As he had learned, it made the media more attentive to his statements and generally gained more ink.

Michael, the reporter, used a hand gesture to Jack to just continue. He also motioned to his photographer partner to start snapping candids.

Jack smiled and understood that this was a chance for him to disparage most of the advertising by his competition. He opined, "I think most advertising is insulting to the intelligence of the average viewer. It's nonsense. Most of it is like Muzak, that unrecognizable noise we sometimes hear in an elevator." The creative director was building up steam. "Get relevant. Get real," he said, as if he were the president of the United States.

The interviewer looked again at his notes. "Many people say your work is all about gaining attention," Michael riposted. "How does that relate to your latest statement about 'Let's get relevant. Get real'?"

Shelly nodded and held up her hand to answer this question. "It's a good question," she responded. "We have a personal philosophy at this outstanding agency."

Suddenly, Jack O'Brien turned his head to her, anxious to hear this never-before announced agency mission.

"So what is the code of this outstanding agency?" Michael asked. "Is it just about being unexpected and outrageous and maybe even a little crazy? We would just like to know."

Jack nodded to the reporter and looked at Shelly. "Me too," he said.

Shelly was good at improvising. She took a deep breath as if she was tired of answering this question and then said, "We do not believe in BS, as my partner has earlier said. However, we do believe in the drama and creativity of television commercials. So we have this theme, which we will put on the walls of the agency in the next week. The words 'The truth … with a twist.'"

Almost immediately, she looked at Jack, who seemed to like the theme and gave her a thumbs-up.

"The truth … with a twist," he repeated, as if he had said it many, many times in the past.

"What's that mean?" Michael, the reporter, asked and motioned for his photographic assistant to take more pictures.

Jack, flummoxed, motioned to Shelly to explain this semiprofound philosophy.

"As my partner said earlier, we do not believe in BS. We like to tell it like it is. If you noticed our new Cannes gold lion, we did just that. We acknowledged that Hooters had better cuisine than you would expect … and better, sexier scenery than most other restaurants. Hence, the line 'Va-va-va- food.'"

"The truth … with a twist," Jack said, as if it was the guiding principle of this rather funny commercial.

"Have you ever been there?" Jack asked the reporter. "It actually features food that makes you smile, and you can quote me on that."

"I've never been there," the photographer jumped into the conversation. "You should go this afternoon," Shelly retorted. "Get the Big Hootie or the Texas Melt. It's amazing. And the Key lime pie is quite a tasty dessert." "C'mon, Michael, don't be a prude. Let's go to the place this evening," Lara, the photographer, suggested.

"I guarantee you will like it," Jack agreed.

Michael Ortiz turned off the recording device and looked as his attractive female photographer.

"You would actually like to go to Hooters with me?" he asked. "Why not?" she answered.

Within minutes, the *Ad Age* couple was out the door for a trip to the local Hooters where they indulged in cheese sticks, some boneless wings, and onion rings. To her credit, Lara took some pictures of the food to underscore the new focus of the restaurant.

You Know Where.
You Know When

After a string of sexy successes, O'Brien, Lipschitz, and Partners was invited to pitch for more mainstream accounts in the hopes the shop could somehow work their magic on more humdrum products.

Thanks to Shelly's Rolodex of pharmaceutical clients, she did get a return call from a Mr. George Claybourne, who presented himself as the marketing director of Anusol.

"Anusol?" Shelly asked ignorantly.

"Well, I will assume from your response that you do not have a problem eliminating stools from your rectum."

"Oy vey," was her rare Yiddish response.

"Of course!" Mr. Claybourne answered. "No one wants to talk about their anus. But this is an affliction that affects 25 percent of all US citizens over the age of fifty. I think your agency could put us on the map and save millions of people who have hemorrhoid pain."

"Why us?" she asked.

"All our traditional agencies ask for a long list of side effects, such as heart attacks, excretion discomfort, and psychological depression due to lack of sex, especially in the anal geography."

"The anal geography," Shelly repeated and giggled like a middle schooler who had just been told her first dirty joke.

"Yes, of course," George answered matter-of-factly. "As sex has become more experimental, anal intercourse has become more popular … but, but, but … rectal inflammation eliminates that option."

"That could possibly be too much information," Shelly responded as a prude, raised by her very middle-class mother.

"That's exactly our problem," George wholeheartedly agreed. "All of our current commercials are about 10 percent information and 90 percent medical disclaimers, which are a complete turnoff to our target audience.

"Let me make this slightly more attractive to your creative agency," the marketing director of Anusol continued. "If we could possibly get advertising on the air that eliminates why *not* to use our very useful Anusol product, we could guarantee an eight-million-dollar advertising budget."

As a savvy ad exec, Shelly wrote down *8* and six zeroes next to it. "Very interesting," she then answered after looking at all those zeroes. "I will bring your proposal up the executive council." As if there was such an upstart committee at the agency.

"Are your fucking kidding me!" Jack O'Brien screamed at the 9:00 a.m. meeting at the agency.

"Eight million dollars," Shelly quietly responded. "Are you fucking kidding me!" Jack repeated.

"Eight. Zero. Zero, Zero. Zero. Zero, Zero," she repeated for emphasis and them slapped the handwritten digits on the table.

"Stop! Stop! Stop!" Jack interrupted.

"It might be interesting to learn more about anal intercourse," the shy British voice intoned from the edge of the table. It was Martin Parsons, the straight-laced, forever-eager, British-born planner.

Jack O'Brien just about had a whiplash as he jerked his head toward the voice.

"We wouldn't lose much from a focus group or two," Shelly encouraged. "It would at least show due diligence if we decide not to pitch this lucrative account." She then pointed again to the handwritten digits on the table.

"Could we film the focus group and then market this bullshit on YouTube?" Jack asked sarcastically.

"That would probably be unethical," Martin, the planner, advised.

"I'm out of here," Jack said and left the morning meeting.

Two weeks later, the agency had recruited eighteen guinea pigs that were over the age of fifty (as per the target audience) and who might be willing to talk about rectal discomfort.

Might is the key word in that last sentence. As Martin, the moderator, soon discovered, it was uncomfortable for this group of strangers to reveal their itches, pains, and ouches.

"For the most part, I just cope," one woman finally volunteered. "Me too," a middle-aged man chimed in.

"Same here," another man agreed.

And then there was silence for at least sixty seconds.

"Are there any treatments that help?" Martin finally asked.

"None that I'd like to talk about," a Latina woman finally said with a shrug.

"It's a very private thing," a man across the table agreed.

That sort of reticence characterized the next fifteen minutes. Martin tried to probe related areas, such as excretions and showers, but the group was primarily mute. In desperation, he finally decided to address the subject of anal intercourse.

"In the butthole?" one man asked incredulously. "Holy shit," one woman objected.

One woman actually pushed her chair back from the table and gathered her belongings to leave the focus group.

Sensing the inevitable, Martin Parsons thanked everyone and announced that this was the end of the focus group session.

Behind the one-way mirror in the adjoining room, Jack O'Brien was farting with laughter. To be honest, so was Shelly Lipschitz, who felt she had just witnessed the most unusual focus group of her life. Tess D'Emelia, O'Brien's art director, was simply shaking her head, wondering what kind of place she had joined. "Yikes," she finally uttered. "I would think the less said the better."

"I completely agree," Jack O'Brien retorted and then gave a thumbs-up gesture to his new art director. "Thank God we hired you, Ms. Pictures."

In the next few days, they had the campaign. And in his presentation to the client, Jack actually used the line Tess had offered after the focus group.

"As my art director told me a few days ago, 'the less said the better.' In consultations with our legal counsel, we have discovered that the woman is brilliant. If we can create a campaign for Anusol that actually never makes a medical claim, we can eliminate fifty seconds of legal disclaimers. This will make you stand out from the pack … and potentially triple your budget and ad exposure, since you won't have to pay for disclaimers.

"Also, what we discovered from our focus groups: no one wants to talk about this particular affliction."

"*Mum*'s the word," Martin chimed in on cue.

"So I would like to introduce my art director partner. Her name is Tess D'Emelia. We basically only have a four-frame storyboard, but hopefully it will speak volumes."

Tess then walked next to Jack and presented the first board. It had only three words, which were arched around a dot—which was strangely wrinkled.

These were the words: You know when.

As Tess held up the visual, Jack hit the button on his audio component. It was a compilation of pain. "Ow, ay, yi, yi. Ouch. No, no. Oh, please."

"Tess, the next frame," Jack encouraged.

The woman confidently presented the bottom part of the previous presentation. It was again a strangely wrinkled circle underscored with three other words: You know where.

Jack again hit the button on his audio machine. "Yes, OK. Smooth."

Jack nodded to Tess to present the next board. It was a close-up of a wrinkled circle with accompanying words on top and at the bottom, passing out of frame.

In her fourth frame, the wrinkled circle came closer to their eyes and accepted the super Anusol.

The committee of the Anusol company watched the presentation in awe. "Wow," George Claybourne involuntarily uttered.

"Could we get this on the air without a major disclaimer?" his legal counsel asked.

"I don't see why not, since we make no actual medical claim," Shelly answered. "And given your eight-million-dollar budget, this might be the most exposed pharmaceutical commercial in the past decade."

Just Put a Band-Aid on It

Johnson & Johnson called the agency with the idea that the agency could perhaps bring some magic to their Band-Aid brand.

"We like that motto of yours in *Ad Age*, 'The truth … with a twist.'" "That's the truth-ish," the receptionist answered, as she had been advised to do so.

"My name is Bernard Williams, and I am the marketing director of the Band-Aid brand. Can you possibly connect me with Shelly Lipschitz, who was recently interviewed by *Ad Age*?"

Within a few seconds, Shelly was on the phone and was advised by the receptionist that this might possibly be a new business call. "Hi, this is Shelly," the chief marketing officer said. "And I am speaking with Mr. Important at J&J?" Over the last few months, she had learned to relax her formal style to be more in keeping with the iconoclastic agency.

"Shelly? Shelly Lipschitz?"

"Speaking!"

"Oh, oh, oh. This is Bernard Williams with J&J, and I thought you might perhaps be able to help us with our Band-Aid brand. To be more precise, I liked what was said about you in the last *Ad Age* article. The profile was called 'The Truth … with a Twist.'"

"That's us," Shelly boasted.

"But right now, that's not us," the prospective client answered. "People think Band-Aids can solve a myriad of maladies—everything from cancer to Alzheimer's disease to gunshot wounds from an AK-47."

"So if I were to get shot this afternoon with an assault weapon, I should *not* treat it with a Band-Aid strip?"

"Hello, are you kidding me?" the prospective client asked.

After a short dramatic pause, Shelly answered, "Yes, of course. I think I understand your dilemma. You wish to extol the amazing advantages of the Band-Aid brand but not over-promise that it will save your life from a heart attack. It cannot cure a heat stroke?"

"No, it cannot."

"It cannot cure diabetes?" "No, it cannot."

"It cannot cure—"

"No, it cannot," the prospective client interrupted. "But I do appreciate your sense of humor. I think you truly do understand our marketing problem. We wish to build up our credentials and market share but tell the truth … with a twist."

"Got it. I love this sort of challenge," Shelly answered. "It's right up our alley."

Quite frankly, the agency struggled about how to present this proposition to the public without denigrating their own product's capabilities.

It was easy to proclaim that Band-Aids wouldn't cure cancer or solve erectile disjunction or even make a migraine headache less critical. But the focus group audience was not idiotic. They instinctively knew that each of these claims were false and imminently rejectable.

The moderator, Martin Parsons, was perplexed but curious. "So what can Band-Aids help?"

"A pinprick," one woman volunteered. "A paper cut," another man answered.

"Maybe a punched pimple," a young woman offered.

After a few minutes to reflect on this clear lack of opportunity, Martin went out on a limb. "What about the earthquake in Haiti? How could Band-Aids help? Anyone? Anywhere please?"

There was only laughter.

After a few more seconds, the British planner became the room's entertainer. "How about the hurricane in Puerto Rico?"

There were a few chuckles but mostly just silence in the room. Encouraged, Martin Parsons stepped further and asked the group if Band-Aids could possibly alleviate mental illness.

The focus group looked at him in stunned silence.

"But if we claimed such miraculous cures, would you consider us nuts or arrogant or just sarcastic?"

"Obviously, it would be just a joke and a rather funny one," the woman who projected this as a good remedy for pinprick suggested.

"It would be absurd and kind of goofy if the brand suggested they could help solve the global warming. That's what so many advertisers do. But with Band-Aid, it would be seen as keen satire. I would probably admire them even more for the irony," another man in the panel said.

"Why shouldn't Band-Aids cure blindness?" one man suggested. Everyone in the room got the joke.

"Hey, why not put on a Band-Aid on our North Korea *contretemps*?" a woman added.

Again, everyone got a chuckle (although few understood the French word *contretemps*).

"Let's put a Band-Aid on Trump," a liberal woman suggested. "I like Trump," a hard-hat right-winger countered.

"OK, no politics," Martin, the planner, signaled a time-out on this topic. "I get it. Don't go overboard as with Trump. But maybe, we could gain ground by claiming that Band-Aids can take credit for world peace."

"Wouldn't that be nice," one woman on the panel laughed and encouraged the room for further worldwide improvement.

"How about the end of global warming?" "How about no prejudice?"

"How about having a decent conversation with your teenage son?" Silence. Then after a few seconds, everyone again laughed.

Martin thanked all the participants for their thoughts and ushered them out of the office. He was immediately compelled to write a précis of his observations.

According the group, the actual usage of the Band-Aid product was insignificant and probably unadvertisable. However, the problems in the world were significant, and J&J wished to take a leadership role in this regard. It could lead to significant sales.

In the next month, the agency created one of their better print campaigns.

They found ugly earthquake visuals in Ecuador. They found visuals of street riots in Russia. They found a photo of a plane crash in India.

Over the visual, the agency pasted a Band-Aid over the disrupted visual with the line "Just Put a Band-Aid on It."

Along with the visual, the copy read, "We are not claiming to cure cancer or insomnia or bloody terrorism. But if you have a paper cut or some minor injury, put a Band-Aid on it."

A few months ago, it won the Steven E. Kelly award for the best print campaign of the year.

I Lost Eighty-Seven Pounds in One Week

When Jack entered the agency at 9:30 a.m. on this particular Monday, he was greeted by his rather robust receptionist, a usually cheery black woman named Naomi Washington.

"Good morning, Mr. O'Brien," she greeted him rather glumly.

Jack O'Brien might have many flaws, but a sense of those around him was not one of them. He tended to have good antennae; he could somehow intuit when someone was not 100 percent on top of their game.

"Hey, what's going on? You are usually Ms. Chirpy and Cheerful," the creative director said.

The receptionist just shrugged.

"Come on, babe," Jack continued. "This isn't just a business. We're all family here."

After a few seconds, Naomi took out a Kleenex and wiped a tear away. "My boyfriend broke up with me last night."

"Ahh, why?"

"He says I am too fat."

Trying to carefully weigh his words and not physically gauge her girth, the man responded, "I would not call you fat. I would call you curvy." He had learned the term by meeting many fat girls who preferred to describe their heft that way.

"Curvy?" Naomi answered with a smile. "Is that good?" "It's a synonym for sexy," the man said.

After a moment of reflection, the receptionist responded, "I think I should call Nutrisystem and lose twenty, thirty, forty pounds."

Jack took a skeptical step back. "You think those claims are true?"

"Of course, I saw it on television," Naomi answered.

"That doesn't make it true," Jack objected. "It may be legally justifiable, but not necessarily true."

Perplexed by her boss's response, Naomi looked downward and sighed. Sensing her dilemma, Jack made an offer. "Naomi, I am going to check out this Nutrisystem program today and see if the agency could somehow benefit from creating something for them. If so, maybe I can get you in their program as a personal favor. No cost to you!"

The last sentence resonated with the receptionist, who tipped up her head and gave that amazing morning smile she usually exhibited.

As the honcho left the reception area and opened the door to his hallway, he stopped and looked back at woman. "Naomi, curvy is good."

The woman actually giggled and found her usual happy demeanor.

When Jack walked down the corridor to his office, he was somewhat perplexed about Naomi's funk. Instead, he made a right-hand turn just to see if Shelly was in her office. Of course, she was. Ms. Industrious almost always started her day before Jack even got on the subway.

"What's up?" Shelly asked.

"You know Naomi at the front desk?" Jack asked.

"Wonderful woman. Cheerful. Bright smile. Love her. She actually sets a positive tone for everyone who comes to this office."

"Well, she wasn't so cheerful this morning."

"So whadya want me to do? Go tell her a joke?"

After a second, Jack took a breath and responded, "No, it's bigger than that. Her boyfriend broke up with her last night and told her she was too fat. So now she wants to join the Nutrisystem diet."

"Wow," Shelly reacted. She shook her head and stared at her business partner. "You may turn you into a more modern sensitive man after all. Wanna Kleenex?"

"No, no, she's just so sad. Not fair."

Shelly had known some people who went on the diet. It seemed to work but hardly as well as they claimed. "Isn't that the one where Marie Osmond asserts that she lost fifty pounds in three months?"

"It's bullshit. Gotta be impossible, unless you had half your body amputated. But I guess when it comes to love and happiness, people will want to believe. I don't want to really do that testimonial stuff, but wait … wait, wait, I've got an idea."

"What? What? What?" Shelly asked with a wink. "I think you may be getting back to your more recognizable diabolical self."

"Shelly, you know Lorne Michaels from *Saturday Night Live*, don't you?" "I have met him at a few parties, and a friend of mine from Princeton is one of the writers on the show."

"I don't really want to compete with the Mormon queen—what's her name? Marie Osmond! And I don't really think Nutrisystem would appreciate our brash style. So here's the idea: we do a one-time-only commercial that runs on *Saturday Night Live*. It's absurd, but it plays to our theme—the truth … with a twist."

"What's in it for them?" the businesswoman asked. "Nothing." Jack laughed.

"Why would Nutrisystem pay a penny to be mocked?"

"They wouldn't have to. It's not a paid media. It's entertainment. Free press. So we do this mock spot. We turn on the PR mavens and again remind everyone that we have the cool factor. A commercial spoof on *SNL* would be repeated dozens of times in the next few weeks, not coincidentally. It would help attract millions of young fatties, and it would cement our reputation as the most irreverent ad agency in Manhattan."

"Your mind works in weird ways," she said with some admiration.

Over the next few weeks, Jack was energized. Every time he would see Naomi in the morning, he would smile and advise her to "lose that schmuck of a boyfriend. If he can't appreciate curvy, he doesn't belong in the game." Tess D'Emelia, his surprisingly adventurous art director, did some central casting for gaunt, perhaps even for ill people who were willing to sit in a hospital bed and scarf down some Nutrisystem diet.

A small ad in *Backstage* merited many offers for an audition. "We are looking for people with medical afflictions for a two-hour shoot. Scale pay grade. If you have an amputated leg, we would be able to pay double scale." Within one casting day at the ad agency, they had their cast.

The script went like this:

"I lost sixty-seven pounds in sixty-three days. True, I had pancreatic cancer, but that Nutrisystem diet kept me going and gave me a tasty hope of life."

A gaunt woman then addresses the camera. "I lost thirty-seven pounds in twenty-five days. OK, OK, OK, I had a very serious stroke and couldn't eat anything other than broth. But once I figured out the real problem, Nutrisystem was really wonderful."

Cut.

"I lost eighty-seven pounds in one week. Just to be perfectly honest, I did have my right leg amputated below the knee. But what a relief that was! And the Nutrisystem diet was outstanding. Really very, very tasty."

At that point, the guest host of *SNL*, Natalie Portman, walked in front of the hospital bed and addressed the camera, "See what Nutrisystem can do for you. And take care of yourself." After a bite of the food on her plate, she ends the spoof spot with an exclamation, "Ooh, that's good, and I already feel I am losing a few pounds, like my hand." She holds up her hospital gown, and it reveals a missing hand.

Not surprisingly, Nutrisystem's legal department called the agency the next day and threatened to sue.

"It's not paid media," Shelly answered, having checked out the loopholes with her legal counsel. "And I'll bet you have gained a bunch of inquiries from people who want to join your program. No need to thank us," Shelly answered and quietly hung up.

After the commercial ran on *Saturday Night Live*, it went viral. Not surprisingly, it garnered more than a million hits and gained some notoriety for O'Brien, Lipschitz, and Partners. Even Naomi at the front desk had seen the commercial and had to laugh.

"You're such a good egg," Jack told her when he saw her smile. I think you are beautiful just as you are. But if you really want to try those Nutrisystem recipes, both Shelly and I have agreed to give you a three-thousand-dollar bonus check, which should cover one year on their program."

"Well, I will take you up on that," the receptionist said and even blew a kiss to the creative director.

Over the next few months, Jack couldn't tell whether Naomi had actually lost even ten pounds. But she did seem happier, and the agency had gained millions of dollars of free publicity for their outrageous satire.

Dave's Day

Partly on the basis of their huge success with Hooters, the Midwestern folks of Wendy's approached the agency for some promotional glitter.

The firm was founded by Dave Thomas, who named the place after his young daughter, Wendy, in Columbus, Ohio, in 1969. As the perpetual number 3 in the fast-food field, it always trailed behind McDonald's and Burger King. But it was normally rated as having fresher, better food. As a matter of fact, one of their previous ad agencies, D'Arcy, actually created a campaign called Wendy's Way. However, somehow, the chain always lagged and was largely outmuscled by their larger fast-food competitors.

After several years of battling the giants, Wendy's decided to ask for further consulting and creative help. As Wendy told her older siblings, "My dad built up this place and maybe should not be forgotten. I just called O'Brien, Lipschitz, and Partners to see if they could memorialize Dad's amazing contribution to this business."

"Isn't that the firm that made up Herbert Hooter?" one of her brothers asked.

"Yes, and it's paid off for them," Wendy answered. "But we don't want them to make up stuff about our dear dad, Dave."

"Please, please, keep it real," all her siblings advised.

At their first agency meeting, Wendy confronted the elephant in the room. "Just to clear the path, isn't this a conflict with your Hooters client?"

"No way," Jack automatically answered.

"Ay, yi, yi, yi …" Shelly demurred. "It's a little tricky. If we can position this as a promotional account in honor of your father and not an ongoing fifty-two-weeks-a-year business, we may be able to get around that."

"I don't see the conflict," Jack again protested. "One is fast food. And as my dear partner said in one of our early meetings with the Hooters folks, the other is boob food."

"I'd rather we don't repeat that anecdote," Shelly said with some embarrassment.

"Well, it is true," Jack protested. "C'mon. Naked Wings? The Big Hootie?"

After a pause, Wendy interrupted the uncomfortable pause. "I can see the difference, if you can."

"We can."

"We can."

Wendy took over the silence. "I want to do something to remind our fast- food fans that dear Dave helped made a difference in the world of fast food. It would never be as fresh. It would never have golden arches. It would never have a clown acting as a surrogate for fast food."

"Tell me about his history," Shelly suggested.

"He was born in the Great Depression, 1932, and started working in the restaurant business as a twelve-year-old at several different chains, McDonald's, Burger King, etc., etc."

"I don't think we want to go into that," Shelly advised.

"And then he built it up and built it up and up from one thousand restaurants to more than ten thousand. His motto? 'Don't cut corners!' That's why every Wendy's hamburger to this day is square, not rounded."

"When did he die?" Jack innocently asked.

"January 9, 2002," his daughter answered, slightly choked up. "And do you remember things from that day?"

"Indelibly, I cried all day and had several Wendy's burgers in his honor."

Instinctively, Jack O'Brien slapped the table for emphasis and knew that was the answer. "Wendy, you have just given the greatest clue to an amazing award-winning campaign. Your dad was born in the Great Depression, but it's a long, long time ago. No one remembers it other than dead people."

"But when your dad died … ? Who among us cannot remember exactly where we were and what we were doing … when JFK was shot, when John Lennon was taken at the Dakota apartments? And when your dear dad, Dave Thomas, passed from this earth, clearly, you remember it as if it was yesterday."

"I still do," she admitted.

"So we will call that Dave's Day, not Dave's Death Day—that's too much.

But we will turn it into an event with maybe 10 percent off on everything." "A one-day event," Wendy asked.

"Maybe not," Shelly joined in and began to improvise. "We could call the Monday the day after Dave's Day and then on Tuesday, the second day after Dave's Day, and the third day after Dave's Day. Probably no more than one week. Because that would not be respectful of your dear dad, Dave."

"And we would never want to do that," Jack offered and completed her sentence.

After another thirty minutes of remembrances, Shelly and Jack escorted Wendy of out their offices as if it were the end of a wake.

Once they walked her to the elevator, the two partners looked at each other. "That was easier than I thought," Shelly quietly said.

"We may need to do three or four commercials for the week of Dave's Day," Jack said with a sigh.

"Once we do the first one, it will be gravy." Shelly smiled.

The first of the series aired on January 8, the day before Dave Thomas's death anniversary. It was basically black and white stock footage of a funeral precession, intercut with glorious food shots of Wendy's quarter-pound singles, baked potatoes, Black Forest ham and cheese, and a frosty.

Over this funeral footage, we heard the voice-over of Christopher Walken: "You probably remember where you were sixteen years ago when you heard the horrible news that fast-food impresario Dave Thomas of Wendy's passed away after providing the best fries, Black Forest ham and cheese, baked potatoes, and the best darn square hamburgers ever made. 'Cut no corners,' Dave would say.

"Let's celebrate Dave's Day tomorrow at Wendy's. Bring in your car, your motorcycle, or your hearse, and enjoy 10 percent off. It's Dave's Day at Wendy's. Let's make it wonderful."

At the end of this script, we do see a procession of hearses going up the drive-up window at Wendy's.

The camera then cuts to the Wendy's logo and the simple words "Dave's Day. January 9. All day."

Two days later, the agency ran another commercial: "OK, maybe you missed Dave's Day on January 8. But at Wendy's, we're so generous we're going to give you another chance. Celebrate the third Dave's Day tomorrow with 10 percent off on Chili Cheese Pasta, Chicken Caesar Wraps, and your favorite soft drinks. Drive up the takeout window in your convertible, bicycle, or commemorative hearse, and enjoy Dave's Day III. We only get the chance to celebrate this food maven's life and death once a year. Let's make it wonderful."

Three days later, the agency ran their third and last commercial of the series. Again, it was Christopher Walken's voice. But in this last spot, the visual was a funeral procession with police stoppage in front of Wendy's, and the entire procession would go to the drive-through window.

Christopher Walken's voice would say, "OK, we are running out of time to celebrate Dave's Day at Wendy's. But you still have this weekend when you can enjoy Turkey and

Swiss, Chicken Grill, Triple Hamburger and Cheese, and your favorite frosty—10 percent off. Dave would like it if you would pay your respects and get a delicious meal in his honor. Live it up. Celebrate his passing. Let's make Dave's Day wonderful."

The verdict: In the *New York Times* advertising column, it was dubbed the most macabre campaign ever seen. "A funeral procession lining up for a fast- food window? Really? For a Wendy's burger? Omigod. What will O'Brien, Lipschitz, and Partners come up with next? Snuff films?"

On the other hand, Wendy's did record a 30 percent increase in sales during the week of Dave's Day. Evidently, the young American consumer gets a kick out of a ghoulish sense of humor.

Inspired by that success, the agency and client did run a rerun of the commercials during Halloween weekend and enjoyed another 20 percent boost in sales.

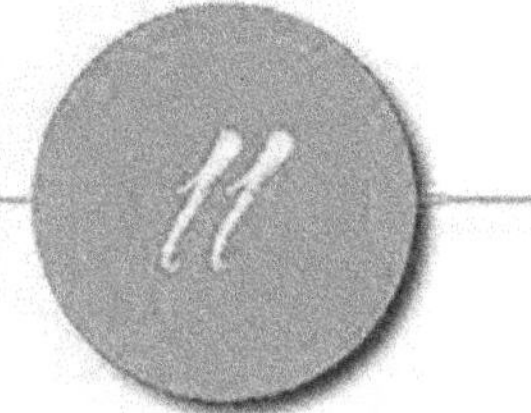

I Dough, I Dough

Ryan had been thinking of the topic after seeing *Black Swan* last weekend. Truth be told, he thought it was a Marvel Comic thriller, only to discover it was a sensitive ballerina love affair story of one woman for another.

Ironically, the guy never really hated chick flicks and actually adored Natalie Portman, but the lesbian attraction made him think twice.

Inspired by his exposure to the other side, he decided to confront his most able partner on the following Monday. "Shelly, I know you are a lesbo …" he began.

"A bad beginning," she corrected him. "It's like calling someone a homo, a dyke, or a gay fuck."

"Fair enough," Jack reacted. He recalled having those learning lessons from the Jesuit priests at Fordham High School. "You can't just stereotype everyone," Father Michaels advised. "A Jew may not be your girlfriend, but you don't need to call her a kike. An Italian worker may not be the most loyal pizza server on Orchard Street, but you shouldn't call him a wop. I could do this African American too, but I should not do so. Be kind. Be fair. Be loving."

"You continue to amaze me," Shelly answered. "What? You want to meet my girlfriend and convert her to the old school?"

"No," Jack said. "I just want to inspire this agency to the next level. We've got enough fast-food and loser brands. And the press gives us the kudos of being on the forefront of the brave new world. But I read the newspapers and listen to the news a few minutes a day. I realize that the world is changing. LGBT is hip," he said reluctantly. "Shouldn't we have an LGBT brand?"

"Other than the fashion brands of Ellen DeGeneres, Anne Hecht, and Lindsay Lohan—like Pretty Pink Pearl, Tomboy Tailors, and Wildfang."

"I don't know those brands," Ryan proudly admitted. Rethinking his initial proposal, Ryan shook his head and said he might not be quite ready for this. "Maybe it's a little too overt and a little too early," he said.

"No, I am proud of you for even bringing up the subject," Shelly responded. "Let me research this. We can find a brand that is LGBT-friendly that might create award-winning advertising, some positive buzz, and also enhance our image as the most contemporary agency in NYC."

Shelly did research the topic and found that Apple, Google, and Nike were prime targets, but her favorite of the bunch was a more obscure brand. She had a hunch that the agency could create breakthrough advertising for Ben & Jerry's ice cream.

"Are they a gay couple?" Jack asked.

"I honestly don't know for sure, but they are from Vermont." "What's that mean?"

"It's a liberal, enlightened state," Shelly answered.

"But if I present a campaign to them, will it be to a group of queers?"

Shelly just blew out a breath of frustration. "Hey, pal, you've got to change your language. And I might add here, so what if they were 'queer,' as you like to say? But they are not! They are both married men with families and are both culturally sensitive to the LGBT community in Vermont and increasingly in America."

"So I could probably relate to them."

Shelly continued, "Other than quiet PR, they have never done even a semiovert LGBT appeal. Within the constraints of mass media, we could be a pioneer, especially with a new brand they just renamed I Dough, I Dough. The package features two chunky monkeys— the previous brand moniker— walking hand in hand on a beach."

"Ich," Ryan instinctively responded.

"I think I should probably handle most of the presentation on this pitch," Shelly reacted.

"I'll work on some breakthrough creative, hopefully with the help of Tess, Martin, and you," he said as he walked out of her office. "But just to remind you that I am not a Neanderthal. I do appreciate and enjoy Elton John."

"That's so brave of you," Shelly said sarcastically and waved goodbye to her business partner as he walked out the door.

The next day, Jack called in his art director, Tess, and his strategic planner, Martin. "Martin, no need to do a focus group on this. I think with your vast contacts in the research field, you can reach a conclusion on this question. What is the reaction of the general public to gay- or lesbian-friendly advertising? Is it a turnoff? Is it a sign of enlightenment? I listen to the news and watch the award shows, so I think it's a more accepted trend. Just spend a few days getting me a topline on this."

"Delighted to do so, Chief," Martin answered and walked away. "I am always happy to do sex-oriented research. If you would like me to run a gay- men group in the agency, I would be more than happy to do so," Martin volunteered.

"Just a topline will suffice," Jack answered.

"Got it. Toodles." Martin waved and swished out of the office.

"OK, here's the deal," Jack offered to Tess. "I want to pitch Ben & Jerry's Ice Cream on an LGBT platform."

"You?" Tess asked skeptically.

"Yes, but actually on behalf of Shelly. I don't want some stupid overt lesbo porn-scene commercial," he instructed.

"Of course not. What's the name of the specific ice cream?" "I Dough, I Dough."

"Lovely," Tess said. "I already have the idea. We just show two women in chaise lounges on a beach in the Bahamas. Remember those old Coca-Cola commercials where teenagers would fall in love over two straws in a glass of Coke? We recreate that with two plastic spoons and one container of Ben & Jerry's. It's sweet. It's innocent. It's loving. It's delicious."

"God damn. That's brilliant. No wonder why I hired you!" he exclaimed. "Let's act like it took us a week to come up with that idea and go to Miami tomorrow."

"I can't. I've got a boyfriend," Tess answered.

"Good to know," Jack answered. "So let's create a storyboard this week."

By Wednesday, Shelly had arranged a presentation for the Ben & Jerry's client in Vermont. But on Thursday, research groups had reported that there was no big downside in today's society to showing hand-holding lesbians (a little dodgier with two male gays). By Friday, Tess had drawn the storyboard of two women sharing a private moment with intercut of the new Ben & Jerry's flavor. Between 3:00 p.m. and 5:00, Jack wrote the copy.

On Monday, the agency presented.

Shelly led off the pitch. "Thank you for inviting us, Ben, Jerry, and the board. We believe you have a wonderful product and a wonderfully enlightened one in today's society. We especially love the fact that you are LGBT friendly, especially as a lesbian in today's business society."

Unaccustomed to not being the lead presenter, Jack joined in. "You bet! Me too!"

"You are a lesbian too?" Ben asked.

"No. No way. But I am definitely sympathetic," Jack shot back. "Continue." Ben motioned.

Shelly took a deep breath and began her prepared speech. "Love is love. There is no difference. If it's between a man and a woman, if it's between a woman and a woman, if it's between a man and a man, or if it's between bisexuals, it's love. And that's the definition of your brand. It's taste, it's satisfaction—it's love. So we have tried our best to capture that emotion, and the payoff is this commercial."

She then tossed the baton to Ryan, who had the good sense to introduce his art director, who had the wisdom to inspire this commercial. "Just like an old- time Coke commercial, it's no different than two attracted people trying to feel even more attracted to each other. In Coke days, it would be about two straws. In today's world, it's no different than two plastic spoons over Ben & Jerry's."

Pausing for some emphasis, Jack took the stage and did his best not to oversell the commercial. "It's a sweet story of love, all food for America and the good values of Ben & Jerry's." He then hit the Play button, and the audience heard the clearly recognizable voice of Ellen DeGeneres.

"It's not strange. It's not unnatural. It's to be shared. I dough, I dough. And to be enjoyed. Thanks to Ben & Jerry's enlightened view of the modern world. Want another spoonful? I dough, I dough.

"So good. So today. So Ben and Jerry's."

The commercial made the headline of the *NY Times* ad column. The banner was positive. "An enlightened LGBT commercial." It saluted O'Brien, Lipchitz, and Partners as perhaps the most attuned advertising agency to connect with a changing world without alienating the rednecks.

That night, Jack celebrated the rave with Shelly and her friend—a woman named Carolyn. He couldn't help but wonder who was the male-ish partner of this relationship but promised himself not to fantasize.

"It's so nice to meet you," Jack extended his hand.

"You didn't bring your boyfriend?" Carolyn innocently asked.

"Not tonight," Jack wisely demurely. "Tonight, I just wanted to meet Shelly's dear heart and perhaps share a couple of cones from the nearby Ben & Jerry's. Have you tried I Dough, I Dough?"

"Not yet." Carolyn giggled.

"Well, as they say in commercials, 'It's so good. So today. And it's to be shared.'"

The two women walked hand in hand to the ice-cream emporium. Jack, having learned his lessons from his dad, walked on the street side of the sidewalk to protect the women. They enjoyed the new flavor. But they did not share spoons.

It's in the Bag

In the next few months, the ad agency did its best to digest the progress of the positive press reports of America's most daring agency. It helped them attract several underdogs, several adventurous clients. But could the same communication philosophy work with prestige clients?

Could it pay off for Mercedes or Emirates Airlines or American Express or Rolex or Tiffany?

In the process of kicking around this topic, Shelly chimed in, "Let's try Tiffany."

"I don't think I have ever been in the store," Jack admitted.

"Of course not. Why would you pay exorbitant prices for the same kind of clothing you can get from J. Crew?"

"Why would anyone?"

"Service, neighborhood, prestige, jewelry, I don't know. But I'll bet Martin would have a field day trying to ascertain why someone would pay more for underwear from Tiffany than from JCPenney."

"Fascinating dilemma," Martin admitted. In his earlier life, he had actually researched Rolls-Royce in London and had a sense for the snob appeal versus insecurity of big-ticket brands.

"It is all about value," Martin predicted to the twosome. "But as the cliché says, value is in the eye of the beholder."

"Is that a commonly known cliché?" Jack asked. "I never heard it before."

"But you know what I mean." Martin tried to explain himself. "Everything is relative."

"I have heard that before," Shelly countered.

Over the next few weeks, while Martin set up a focus group of affluent buyers, Shelly checked her contacts for any decision makers at Tiffany's. It took a while and a few cross-references to identify a Mr. J. Pierpont Morgan, who was identified as the chief communication officer of Tiffany & Co.

"May I call you, J. Pierpont?" Shelly asked in her phone call to Tiffany's two days later.

"Yes. That's fine. Feel free to call me J. Pierpont," the man answered with a faux British accent.

After a private chuckle, Shelly asked the man if he was in charge of advertising.

"We prefer to call it communications," he admonished. "So do we," Shelly answered.

"Are you a regular customer of Tiffany's?"

"I go there when I need a nice present for someone."

"Like most people," the man agreed.

Shelly took a deep breath and launched into her pitch. "Our goal would be to get people to visit your fine store more frequently and perhaps spend more money when they do visit."

"A good goal," the man answered.

"May I send you some examples of our communications and successes and perhaps exchange contact information?" the woman asked.

"Of course," J. Pierpont responded. "And I look forward to meeting you in person."

It was perhaps the shortest cold call she had ever made. After she hung up, she stared at the phone for a few seconds. It wasn't necessarily a bad call, just distant. Well, maybe that would change when they could meet in person and see the miraculous creative work.

In Martin's focus group, there was a group of ten middle-aged women who were chatty, almost as if they knew each other. They didn't, of course. But they had so much in common, you could easily mistake them for next-door neighbors from the Upper East Side.

"I love the place," one woman explained. "I feel as if I am always treated with respect there. That's a rare trait these days."

"Does it feel old-fashioned?" Martin probed.

"Not at all!" another woman objected. "It's au courant, darling."

"No one is ever disappointed with a gift from Tiffany's," another woman chimed in.

"It's *bellisimo*." "It's *sine qua non*." "It's *perfecto*."

Martin had rarely heard such a barrage of foreign idioms in any focus group. Just to change the tempo, he reached under the table and brought out a small Tiffany's bag. Of course, it was that familiar teal color, but what struck the moderator was the instant reaction of all the women. They looked at the package as if it were the most valuable Christmas gift of all time.

"Omigod, it's my favorite bag of all times!" one wide-eyed woman exclaimed.

"It's says cache," another woman nodded.

"If I am carrying that bag on Fifth Avenue, I automatically get a cab before anyone else," the woman to Martin's right admitted.

"Or maybe a limo," another woman shrugged in jest.

Sensing the trend, Martin reached for the bag and rotated it on the conference room table. "This bag is somehow special? It speaks to you? When you are carrying that Tiffany's bag, you feel somehow superior?"

"I don't know if I would go that far," one woman answered.

"I would," another answered.

"I do," another woman responded.

"What? Would you rather be carrying a Macy's bag?" a woman at the far end of the table asked sarcastically.

Instantly, the table erupted with uproars of laughter. It was as if they heard the funniest line of all times, as if Groucho Marx or Dave Chappelle or Louis C.K. was in the room.

"Ladies, ladies, ladies, that's enough for one day." From several years in the business, he had learned when and how to end a session such as this. "If anyone wishes to take the Tiffany bag to get a taxi or a limo, help yourself." Instantly, four or five hands reached across the table to take the package.

Watching this spectacle from the one-way mirror, Shelly commented on her confidence of winning this account. "It's in the bag," she uttered.

"That's the line." Jack slapped his knee and agreed.

"Will you give me credit?" the woman asked.

"Never!"

"You are such a prick!"

"Yes, but we are going to win this account," Jack high-fived his favorite business partner of all times.

After establishing the theme-line thrust, it was a fairly easy job to create the storyboard. Given the stakes, Tess drew up some frames but suggested it might be more effective to actually gain some street footage of customers walking with the famous Tiffany's bag.

It was not too difficult to stage. She had ten Tiffany bags and gave them out freely to people for a one-hundred-dollar cash payment.

We see a woman with a baby carriage and a Tiffany bag in hand.

We see a man and woman kissing in Central Park. He extends his Tiffany bag to the woman.

We see a mom at the graduation of her high school son. We see a great-grandmother placing the bag in a baby crib.

We see a military guy coming back from a war, greeted by his wife with a Tiffany gift.

We see a woman with a Tiffany bag easily able to hail a cab.

We see a diseased man in the hospital with a seventy-something woman at his side, giving him a Tiffany package.

We see two teenagers in Manhattan—the woman is giving the boy a Tiffany package. He can't wait to open it.

Against this edited visual, the agency hired Tom Hanks to record the following: "Will you ever be happier? Will it be true love? Will graduation lead to bigger and better things? Will you find peace? Will he ever know how much you admire him?

"Life is full of questions, but for the really important ones, there's a simple, meaningful positive response. Will I be pleasantly surprised? (*Pause.*) It's in the bag."

When the agency presented their prototype commercial to J. Pierpont Morgan, he watched it carefully and ultimately had tears in his eyes. "That's exactly the way I feel about Tiffany & Company. It's as if you read my mind. How soon can we run it?"

Shelly was smiling. "We just need to make sure we have legal clearance for all the people portrayed in the video."

"In time for graduation?" he asked.

"In time for summer weddings," Tess offered.

"In time for family reunions," Jack said.

"In time for anniversaries," Martin joined in.

"I do love it," J. Pierpont Morgan said and brought in five Tiffany Bags for the presenting crew.

"It's rush hour. Do you think I will be able to get a cab?" Shelly mused. "Just hold this very recognizable teal-colored package and wave to oncoming yellow taxis. The answer to your question? It's in the bag."

Cowboy Vodka

It was a call out of nowhere. A man named Butch Rogers called the agency and asked to speak with someone who might be able to create an award- winning advertising. Naomi, at the front desk, took the call and tried to connect with Shelly or Jack, but both were out of the office. In desperation, she tried Ryan O'Brien's office, and as luck would have it (or not), he was in.

"Ryan, can you take a call from a new business prospect?" "Absofuckinglutely," he responded.

After a few seconds, the call was connected, and the two men introduced themselves. Butch presented himself as the marketing director of Tito's Vodka. "I have been following your agency for the past several months and have admired your courage in breaking with tradition. That's in our DNA here in Austin, Texas, where we handcraft the product."

"Tito's?" Ryan O'Brien asked.

"Tito's," Butch answered.

"I love that brand! I have at least one glass on the rocks every night, after putting in a full day here at O'Brien, Lipschitz, and Partner. I used to enjoy Stoli or Smirnoff, but lately, I have become more patriotic to the USA."

"That could be our angle," Butch jumped in.

"You betcha," Ryan said, trying to sound like something like a country boy.

Sensing some compadre sentiment, Butch announced his ambitions, "We came from nowhere, and we are now the number 6 top-selling brand in America."

"Well, maybe with our help, you become number 3 or 2."

"Or number 1!" Butch countered.

'That's the spirit," Ryan applauded. "I'm going to send some materials and get the squad working to make you number 1. You're in Austin, right?"

"Right."

"Great city. Great music. Great vodka. Come visit."

"I definitely will, but meanwhile, I'm going to send some stuff from the agency and get the gang on the case."

That afternoon, he gathered Jack, Shelly, Martin, and Tess and explained this wonderful opportunity. To kick off the topic, he had five glasses filled with ice and then presented the bottle.

"It's a great, amazing brand created by a couple of cowboys in Texas. It's called hand-made. Within the past two decades, it has become the number 6 brand in America. It will be number 1 in the next few years, with our help or without us.

"I spoke with the marketing director this morning. He wants to work with us." Ryan then poured a jigger of Tito's in each glass and passed it around the table. "Cheers," he toasted the room as if it were a forgone conclusion that they would become the agency of record for this prospect.

"It's pretty good," Tess said. "I think my young friends all drink it, unless they are having beer."

"Not bitter, kind of sweet," Shelly admitted. "That's because it's made from corn, not potatoes."

"What's *handmade* mean?" Martin asked, looking at the label.

"Well, that's a little bone of contention. They started it in a still in Austin, Texas, and a few other vodka competitors have challenged the claim. But Tito's have won over every legal battle for the handmade claim."

"What do they want?" Jack asked.

"Award-winning advertising," his dad answered. "Who doesn't?"

"Who's their competition?" Shelly asked.

"Mostly all imports," Ryan admitted. "Stoli from Russia. Finlandia from guess where. Grey Goose from France. Absolut from Sweden. Ours would be the only one in the top 10 that is batch-made in the US."

"Wow," Shelly said with some surprise. "I would think that may provide as much lever-age in today's world as handmade."

"There might even be a way to combine it with Americana," Jack offered optimistically.

"Where's it made?" Tess asked. "Only one place: Austin, Texas."

"I hear that's a great city," she added.

"Yeah, if you like cowboy boots, country music, and horses," Shelly said sarcastically and got a few laughs from the New York ethnocentric group.

"This will be fun," Jack promised.

The ultimate solution combined three themes—handmade, proudly homemade (as in the USA), and very symbolically American. Usually, that's too many themes for a thirty-second commercial, but Jack promised that this could be weaved and perhaps be delivered in a seamless, even funny way.

Key to this approach in his mind was the quintessential American hero, and in his mind, no one represented that more than the American cowboy. Besides, he argued, it tended to give the brand some heritage (as opposed to a brand created in the past few decades). "Think of the impact of John Wayne, Clint Eastwood, Jeff Bridges, Butch Cassidy, and the Sundance Kid, even Woody from *Toy Story*. They all represent Americana every bit as much as the Statue of Liberty."

"Wouldn't it have to be a modern-day cowboy?" Tess asked.

"Absolutely! Some stud in his twenties who can speak English, French, Swedish, Russian, etc.," Jack teased.

Shelly, accustomed to this drum roll of a presentation from her creative partner, asked him to roll forward.

"OK, here is the basic idea …" Jack was dying to unfold the scenario. "We see our cowboy hero on a Western horse. He's a modern-day Clint Eastwood—cowboy hat, boots, and all. As he strolls down the Champs-Élysées, he discovers a man in a beret, drinking a glass of Grey Goose. We can see the bottle. Our cowboy hero slows his horse down and asks the man in French, "Is it homemade?" The Frenchman laughs and waves him away in that French put-down style. Dissolve.

We see our cowboy now walking through the Fjords of Finland. He finds two people in heavy coats drinking Finlandia. Our cowboy asks the same question, "Is it homemade?" The sophisticated couple responds "no way" and shushes him away. With respect, he does move on. Dissolve.

In the next scene we see our cowboy hero enter Red Square and see some Russian soldiers drinking Soli. Again, we can see the bottle. "Is it homemade?" our cowboy asks, this time in Russian. In retaliation, the soldiers reach for their guns, and our cowboy gallops off, unharmed. Long dissolve.

We see our lonely cowboy in the plains of Texas. As he trots along, we hear some Austin country music with the voice-over of someone who sounds very much like Jeff Bridges.

"At the end of the day, there is only one. One American vodka brand that is handmade deep in the heart of Austin, Texas. One that is brewed in old stock pots and taste-tested six times. One that is now the most favorite American vodka brand and one that easily competes with all the overseas also-rans. Tito's." Cut.

The Frenchman doffs his beret and puts on a cowboy hat as he tastes a shot. "Bon."

The Swedish couple dons cowboy hats, tastes, and says, "Bien, bien." The Russian soldiers take the cowboy hats and sip. "Ya, ya, ya, ya!"

In an ending scene, we see our cowboy hero place the Tito's bottle on the Russian table. As he does so, a cowboy hat is thrown into the scene next to the bottle. Over that, we see the super.

We see the word *handmade* at the top of the screen. That is then replaced with two lines: Cowboy Vodka. It is then overridden by an overlarge super of the word *Tito's*.

Against this final visual, we hear a rather patriotic country tune—strictly instrumental, not a jingle. Perhaps in the background, we see the cowboy galloping off into the sunset.

After this presentation, the client, Butch Rogers, admitted, "It's not what I expected from your agency. I thought you might stress the handmade attribute.

"Easy enough to do," Shelly responded. "But we ended up thinking that the Americana aspect of this brand—particularly the handmade Americana aspect—gives us a supreme advantage, especially in our nationalistic mood. Otherwise, you might end up competing with homemade vodka made in Iowa or Oklahoma or Santa Fe."

"You've got a point," he admitted.

"And the cowboy thing is huge," Jack joined in. "Let me ask you something. Does Tito Beveridge, who founded this amazing enterprise, wear cowboy boots every day?" Jack knew the answer, having studied the website and every picture of the bio. The founder was never in a Brooks Brothers suit.

"He does," Butch answered, "and occasionally a cowboy hat."

"So own it." The creative director slapped the table. "Nothing says self- sufficient, and perhaps even homemade, more than the American cowboy."

"Interesting insight," Butch said without much commitment. "This is a great city," Tess volunteered.

"And a great product," Shelly continued the roll.

"And a great symbolic story," Jack joined in with another slap on the table. It came off as a crescendo, however just short of a rehearsed theatrical pitch. After this bang-bang sales pitch, there was an odd silence. Butch, the client, looked across the table at the only silent member of O'Brien, Lipschitz, and Partners—the gray-haired chairman emeritus named Ryan O'Brien, who had taken his first call.

"What do you think, Mr. Wisdom?" he asked Ryan.

"I think …" And the old man had learned how to pause for emphasis. "I think … it's brilliant. If you only want handmade, you can go to a million agencies that will give a mac-ramé logo. But it ain't Texan. And it ain't you. And it will not compete internationally." After a pause, the old man knew to not oversell. "That's what I think."

"I knew I liked this old codger from my first conversation," Butch said and bowed to the oldest man in the agency. "I say we give it a shot for a year and see how it goes."

All the younger members of the agency team smiled and tried not to high- five each other. By contrast, Ryan O'Brien, who had bought a tourist cowboy hat in the airport and wore it throughout the presentation, took off his hat, and tossed it across the table toward the bottle. It could have been the final logo shot: Tito's. Cowboy Vodka.

O, Yes

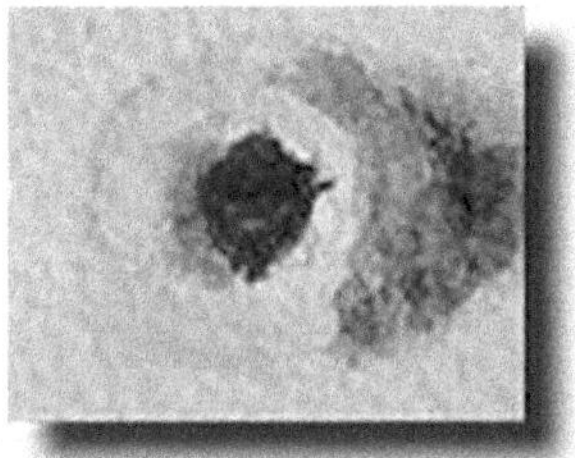

Ever since she was a little girl, Tess D'Emelia loved starting her day with a bowl of Cheerios. Her fondest memories were enjoying a few tales and strawberry-laden crunches with her dad before her school bus came, and she would race outside the door in her Catholic school uniform.

"I love that brand," she told Jack one morning. "Can we gain it and make my dad proud of me?"

"He's not?"

"Yes, of course he is, but this would be icing on the cake."

Jack and Shelly discovered that it was a General Mills brand in Minneapolis. They also discovered that there had recently been a brouhaha about a recent Cheerios commercial that featured an interracial couple sharing a bowl of Cheerios at the breakfast table.

"Was your dad black?" Shelly asked with some sense of humor.

Somewhat upset by bigotry of the boycott, Shelly understood that business was business, and the world was changing, even in the Upper Midwest. "If we focused on the product rather than user imagery, I'll bet we could gain this account," she predicted.

What Jack had learned from his early days in advertising is that if you look at the product long enough, you can find an intrinsic point of difference. With this brand, it was easy. It's in the unique shape of the product.

Yes, there are a few other circular shaped brands—apple chips, Oreos, vanilla wafers, Chips Ahoy!, Big Macs, but few have the pedigree of America's beloved breakfast cereal.

Jack placed ten to fifteen Cheerios on his desk, and it looked like half of a tic-tac-toe board. On a more positive note, it did suggest a campaign.

"*O* what?" he wrote on a Post-it Note as an inspiration and then stuck it to his computer screen. He then emailed notes to all his partners to contribute to this effort.

"I think we have the opportunity to create a very memorable campaign for Cheerios." He then included a close-up of the Cheerio and asked his staff to complete the sentence. "Examples: 'Oh, what a beautiful morning.' 'Oh, yes.' 'Oh, dear, give it thirty minutes of your time.' I've got a good hunch this could be breakthrough."

Within the next twenty-four hours, he had thirty nominations. He thought of creating a song of the litany but ultimately decided it would be better, easier, and cheaper to just create a voice track. With Tess's help, they decided to create a visual of *O* Cheerios that would then be enhanced with letters that would complete the sentiment.

Some would be individual Cheerios plopping into a fresh bowl of milk. Some would be placed on a white background. Some would be shot on a kitchen table.

In conjunction with all these *Os*, they had invited the creative contributors to record their observations about Cheerios.

The track went like this:

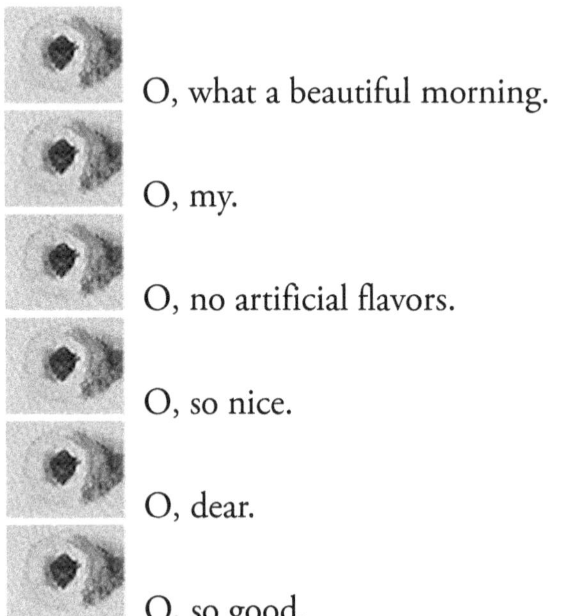

O, what a beautiful morning.

O, my.

O, no artificial flavors.

O, so nice.

O, dear.

O, so good.

O, no artificial colors.

O, migod.

O, ooh-la-la.

O, so delicious.

O, dear.

O, no artificial colors.

O, so natural.

O, no gluten.

O, boy.

O, yes.

O, yes.
(Cheerios are poured in bowl of milk.)
O, O, O, Cheerios.

O, yes.

Within weeks, the commercial became something of a sensation on the air. It was the *New York Times*. It was applauded in as an "enlightened, product-centered commercial."

The next week, Tess bought fresh strawberries and a box of Cheerios.

She made the trek to Brooklyn to share a bowl with her dear father.

As Eddie Fisher used to sing, "Oh, my Papa / No one could be so gentle, and so lovable / Oh, my papa / He always understood."

Instead of singing to the song to her day, she just shared the bowls of Cheerios and gave him the biggest hug, hoping that somehow he would understand her love.

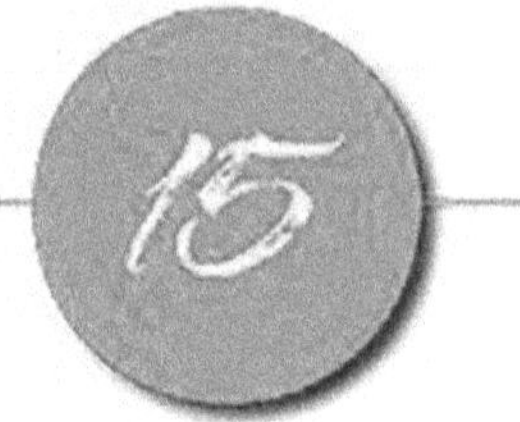

M&M&M&M's

For some inexplicable reason, the agency always had open bowls of M&M's throughout the shop. Perhaps it was a holdover from Ryan O'Brien's earlier days as an account guy on the brand. Or perhaps it was just a sugar-laden jump start for the creative staff to come up with something clever and avoid the after-lunch slump.

After popping one in her mouth, Shelly told herself that this should definitely be one of the agency's brands. Just to prepare herself for a pitch, she goggled the ten funniest M&M Super Bowl commercials. They were amazingly bad. As a matter of fact, she didn't smile one time. The commercials were all goofy M&M cartoon characters, with humor aimed at eight-year-olds.

Shelly came into Jack's office and placed a single M&M on his desk. "It's pretty," he responded.

"We can do better than they have done in the last decade," she declared.

"We always can," he bragged.

Surprisingly, the agency struggled to come up with a campaign that lit anyone's fire. They explored a concept called mindless munching. True to the shop, it spiced up visuals of Ronald Reagan, Vladimir Putin, Albert Einstein, Bruce Springsteen, and Donald Trump. "Too vapid." Shelly frowned, perhaps because of the last image.

They then tried to extol the quality of their chocolate with the line, "Chocolate from Mars." To be honest, Jack O'Brien really liked the spot. It showed an astronaut getting out of his space capsule and discovering a bag of M&Ms on the surface of the alien landscape. The explorer tries to pop one in his mouth, but it keeps ricocheting off his helmet.

Upon looking at the footage, Martin remarked, "Wait, wait, wait! That's not Mars. It's the moon!"

"What's the difference?" Jack asked.

"One is close, one is far. One is red, the other is white. One is a planet in the solar system, the other is a satellite. Most importantly, the man with the helmet only got to the moon, not to Mars."

"OK," Jack interrupted. "Enough science."

Rarely stumped, the agency struggled over the next few days. They tried an effort called the color of taste. Then an indulgent campaign called Make Yourself Happy.

"No, no, no," Jack wisely demurred. "This is an iconic brand. It's like Coca-Cola. Hallmark. The Yankees. It's up there with the best of the best. I can't treat this like Cheetos."

Admonished, the staff tried to scribble ideas over the next few days.

Ironically, once upon a noonday stroll, Martin went into an art gallery in Chelsea and was struck by a piece of art inspired by the Mars confection. The strategic planner stared at the piece for about five minutes and read the complete list. *This might spark something back at the agency,* he told himself.

Generously, he bought the original and a few giclée prints, which he could display in the agency in the hopes that it could possibly inspire the staff to be both visual and verbal.

Jack, Shelly, and Tessa did backflips about the art. As a matter of fact, they contacted the gallery and gained permission from the artist to feature it in their print campaign. The spreads ran in *New York Magazine*, *People*, *Time*, *Harper's*, *Sports Illustrated*, and *Entertainment Weekly*. Just to give the brand an urban edge, they also ran it in on bus shelters, subways, and trains in Chicago and New York City.

The Mars client in Chicago unanimously approved the effort. Forrest Mars asked the agency what they might suggest for TV.

Jack expected the question but had a surprising, atypical answer. "Don't know yet. I actually think it might be distinctive to kick this off with print or outdoor or transit ads. Courageous. Unique. As special as an M&M's."

"Hmm, I sort of admire that," Forrest Mars answered. "Courageous."

The print campaign did gain a lot of attention and very positive press reviews in *Ad Age*. "Just when we thought that all O'Brien, Lipschitz, and Partners wanted to do was create goofy TV spots, they shock up with one of the most elegant print campaigns in years. It's for M&M's.

"And by the way, kudos to the Mars client, who actually had the vision to kick off an admirable campaign on a piece of paper."

Match

Jack worked late hours and was never much of a social butterfly. However, at the age of thirty-one, he sometimes wished he had a main squeeze. The man was thin enough and decent looking but tended to want to talk about advertising all night. For many women, that's not an attractive trait.

After months of going back to his solo apartment and vegging out on the news or ESPN, he decided he should perhaps try to somehow make contact.

It was different from when he was in college, when he and his friends would just hang out in a pickup bar and flirt with each other. It would usually end up in easy sex, but today, everyone was more cautious, including Jack.

After a few too many lonely nights at P. J. Clarke's, he asked a few of his friends how they met women in this day and age. His best friend Chaz suggested, "At work." Jack instinctively knew that was not for him, especially in today's environment. A few of his other friends offered safer routes to find a possible mate.

"Everyone I know over the age of twenty-nine seems to be on Match.com," his buddy Eddie said. "It's a little hit and miss, but unless you want to hang out in a bar, it's the only game in town," his other buddy, Carl, added. "It's a little time-consuming, but there are a lot more women on-site than men, so you get lots of choices. You buy some of your favorites a cup of coffee or a glass of wine and try your best to be entertaining and thoughtful on your first date and try not to get too sexually overt."

"Sounds like a roulette." Jack shrugged.

"It's like a new business pitch. You do it all the time," Carl opined.

"Check it out. What do you have to lose?" his friend Eddie chimed in.

That night, Jack did go on the site. He found three of four good pics of himself—thoughtful, active, laughing, etc. And then he wrote a creative profile of what he liked to do and what he looked for in a woman. Not so complicated. Then he hit the Send button.

By the next day, he had ten winks and ten interested emails. He responded to several of the women and agreed via emails and phone conversations to get together at least for a hello.

That rate of return continued most days. Sometimes, he would prefer to have an actual dinner. After several dates, there were some that progressed beyond casual greetings. In fact, with a few, Jack did have sexual relations. However, he found that somewhat complicated. Unlike his early twenties, when sex meant nothing, by now it seemed to instantly signify a serious relationship. Truth be told, Jack wasn't sure he really wanted an exclusive one-on-one relationship. At this point, it was just more satisfying to play the field.

He did find the contacts from women both exhausting and addictive, but it admittedly beat the alternative of sitting alone in his apartment or alone on a solo barstool. It didn't take him long to figure that he was the right man to pitch the entire Match.com business and bring his creative magic to their television advertising.

Of course, he discussed this with Shelly and Tess and was surprised that they were supportive and even proud of him for getting out there. "It's a big business," Ellie believed. "And given your personal experience, we might be able to win it."

He also brought in Martin, the strategic planner, to try to better understand the reluctance of some to join, along with the fears and pitfalls.

In both the male and female focus groups, there were a few stories of lucky love, but most participants did underscore that it was a fair amount of work.

"A lot of the men lie about their success," one woman said. "A lot of the women lie about their age," a man countered.

"And things that look good on paper, or even on the phone, are completely different when you spend a lunch or a dinner with them." Everyone agreed.

"It's a roll of the dice," one guy admitted.

"Yeah, but it's the only way these days. What are you going to do? Try to hit on your secretary? Or come up to some guy in the subway and say, 'You look like you might wish to have a relationship with me'?" Everyone in the room had a good laugh.

Behind the two-way mirror, Jack became more and more convinced that it was a potential backfire to suggest that Match.com could lead to marriage. Given his own experience and some conversation with his dates, he truly understood that many don't have that as a goal. They just want a match. Maybe a travel companion. Someone to share a movie or a play. Someone to break the tedium of loneliness.

Ahh, the tedium of loneliness, he repeated to himself and took note of his observation on one of those yellow lined legal pads.

"But that just comes off as a downer," he told his two female partners. "Not necessarily," Tess answered. "It takes courage to give it a whirl." "And a sense of adventure," Shelly agreed. "That alone is confidence building."

"It's a complicated topic," Martin, the oracle of the obvious, joined in. "From my experience, people in the focus groups didn't want to feel lonely or desperate. They want to feel proactive, but they are well aware of the odds. Interesting dilemma."

"Let me give this a think over the next few days," Jack offered.

A few days later, he came back with a very unusual script with Tess's art direction help.

It begins with a thirtysomething woman looking through a door peephole to see if someone is at her apartment door.

A few seconds later, she looks again. Again, no one. And again.

Against this visual, we hear the smart, sympathetic voice-over of someone who sounds like Susan Sarandon.

"Do you really believe that Prince Charming is going to come knocking on your door out of nowhere?"

The woman looks again through the peephole.

"Of course, you don't. But you are smart enough, savvy enough, and courageous enough to understand that any relationship is a two-way street.

"Go ahead. Join Match.com. "We are proud of you. Join the twelve million people who wish to discover what else is out there. And good luck."

The male version had a similar psychology. It shows a thirtysomething attractive-enough guy at the Union Square Park all by himself. Yes, he has his computer, but he is totally distracted and attracted by the beautiful woman walking past him.

A beautiful woman does not look back at him. He goes back to his laptop. Same story. And again.

Against this visual, we hear the smart, sympathetic voice-over of someone who sounds very much like Ryan Gosling.

"What? What do you think? Some woman like Cinderella is going to walk out of a fairy tale and put her glass slipper on your lap?"

Our actor looks again at another woman who passes by.

"C'mon. You are too smart for that. It doesn't happen that way. But you are smart enough, adventurous enough, and courageous enough to understand that any relationship is a two-way street.

"Go ahead. Be Brave. Join Match.com."

"Join the twelve million people who wish to discover what else is out there.

And good luck."

The Match.com client approved the work, despite some concerns that it may not be "happy ending" enough. However, they did trust the agency's knowledge and insight on the account.

The next week, *Ad Age* saluted the agency with a rare accolade. "We are constantly getting readjusted to this unpredictable agency. Here's a campaign we rarely see: one that doesn't overtly brag about their (or their client's) success. Instead, they salute the bravery of the people who wish to simply connect with another human being. Humble. Honest. Very, very human. Bravo."

The next day, Jack's Match.com client called him to congratulate him on his enlightened campaign. Within two weeks, he called back to say their subscriptions had increased 25 percent.

A few weeks later, Jack was back to answering his incoming emails from Match.com. One of those contacts would lead to amazing sex, but true to his new business pitch, he called it quits after a one-night stand.

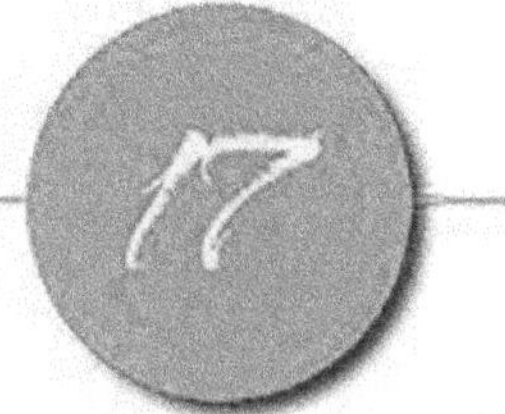

Staples Makes It Possible

Lately, Shelly Lipschitz had begun to accept that more employees worked from home. She had three other people in her account management department who were on the premises only about 50 percent of the time. Two of them were women with young children, who could just as easily complete their work from their home office while nursing a baby. The third was just a guy who simply used this as an excuse to work a few days in his PJs or go to the Belmont racetrack.

Jack had noticed the same phenomenon in the creative department. For many years, many writers and art directors freelanced and would only come into the office a few days a week. Increasingly, all music was done off- campus and usually recorded without a Carnegie Hall studio. (Hey, every twenty-three-year-old music maven can lay down his own track and present it with precision on line.)

Yesterday, when Shelly got a call from Staples to pitch their account. She asked about their perceived point of difference.

"No one goes in the office anymore. Have you noticed?" Carol Barry parried. "In today's world, everyone wants to be an independent entrepreneur and create their own self-made work. So much for teamwork." She sighed.

"I know the trend," Shelly admitted. "Give me figures," Shelly added.

"In 2011, thirty-four million Americans worked out of their own home. In 2016, that number almost doubled to sixty-three million people."

"Egads," Shelly used a word her mother used to utter. "How can we change this?"

"We can't. It's the tech revolution. If you have a computer and a cell phone, and maybe Skype, you can easily work from home. But at Staples, we can take advantage of this business trend since we largely supply home offices."

Shelly's next question was an obvious one. "Why doesn't your current agency do this for you?"

"Right now, we only have a promotional agency for flyers and weekly sales. But given the trends, I just thought it would be advantageous for us to put a stake in the ground and own working from home," Carol, the prospective client, explained further. "I'm relatively new here after a career at Home Depot, but I follow advertising and have been impressed with your agency's out-of-the-box thinking. Interested?"

"Definitely," Shelly answered. "It will take us about a month or so to suss things out, but after that, we will present you a campaign that will knock your socks off and probably persuade more than half of my own employees to work even more from home.

"Well, it's the way of the world, and you can't fight progress," Carol responded. "But with Staples, they will have all the supplies they need for a bang-up job. I look forward to hearing from you for a presentation date. And if you have any questions …" Blah, blah, blah. The two women exchanged contact numbers, and both looked forward to the upcoming weeks.

Shelly couldn't wait to get into Jack's office and announce this exciting new business opportunity. "It's perfect. It will help cement our image as the agency that deals with cutting-edge issues."

Tess also was energized. "Several of my art director friends actually work from home. They love the independence but sometimes miss the office camaraderie."

Jack listened to the opportunity and suggested a line, "When you want to work from home."

Shelly looked at him with a skeptical eye. "Jack, I think we can do better than that. What do you think, Tess?"

"We can try."

"The truth … with a twist," Shelly reminded the team of their agency's motto.

Unfortunately, their initial work had no twist. It was basically a litany of office supplies summed up with the line "Hey, we work from home."

"I am bored to tears," Jack admitted. "Got it. They have copy paper. They have Xerox machines. They have brightly colored folders and file cabinets. Tell me something I don't know."

"We need to somehow capture the consequences and the advantages of owning this trend," Tess suggested.

"You're pretty smart. You should run an agency someday," the creative director proffered.

"Maybe I will someday, if I can work from home," she cleverly countered.

From that, the two of them spun scenarios and success stories of people who work from home.

The first one was the story of a work-at-home dad, despite the trend being largely female. The scene captures a man, a woman, and a young baby in the kitchen at 7:15 in the morning.

The script goes like this:

Wife: What's on your schedule today? Husband: Work.

Wife: Got to go to the office?

Husband: Yes, but not *the* office. The one eighteen feet away from the kitchen. I think I got everything I need from Staples.

Wife: So why are you wearing a tie? Husband: Force of habit.

Wife: Throw it away. You don't need it when you work from home. Husband: Come visit me later on.

Over the next several scenes, we see the husband on phone calls, computer, even Skype. Eventually, his wife comes in with the baby in a carriage.

Husband: Can I walk her? Wife: Sure.

Husband: I'll just take fifteen to twenty minutes. Can you mind the phones while I'm gone? If I get any calls, just them I'll return it in a few minutes when I am out of the bathroom.

Over the next several scenes, we see the dad skipping along with his little baby girl and rejoining his wife at the home office.

Father: Any calls? Wife: None.

Father: I guess I should make a few calls.

As the wife leaves, she throws him a kiss, and even the baby waves to Dad. VO: There are so many advantages to working from home. And Staples, more than any other store, makes it possible. By the way, lose the tie.

Father (on the phone): Yes, of course, I am here. Am I too casual for you? Just kidding. Title: Staples makes it possible. And yes, lose the tie.

The second commercial presented was even more popular, probably because it was even more unexpected.

It opens on a train platform at Hastings-on-Hudson or Dobbs Ferry, New York, at morning rush hour. The train platform is eerily empty. Yes, there are a few octogenarians and teenagers boarding the train, but very few workers.

Train ticket taker (talking to his buddy) outside the train: What's going on here? Last year, we had at least thirty, forty, fifty women boarding this train for a workday in Manhattan. Now, there's no one.

The commercial quickly cuts to several women working from home in front of their computers, answering phones, etc. (sometimes with a baby next to them).

Train ticket taker: Are our prices too high?

Train ticket taker buddy: I don't think price has anything to do with it.

While the train ticket taker looks at a basically empty Metro-North car, we hear a voice-over from someone who sounds remarkably like Frances McDormand.

"Guys, get over it and enjoy the fact that in today's world, more and more women can work at home. Thanks to all the things they can get from Staples—copy paper, tech stuff, you know. It makes life easier for everyone. Well, mostly everyone. In fact, the work-at-home folks have doubled in the past few years. So, hey, get with the system."

Cut back to the empty train station. The Metro-North train ticket taker calls out to empty platform. "All aboard! Last call to the morning train to Grand Central."

Not surprisingly, no one enters. Our ticket taker looks at his buddy and shrugs with a new thought. "Should we go to Staples and figure out a way to work from home?"

As the subway doors start to close, Mitch jumps back on the train and hears the advice of his assistant: "I don't think that's possible."

Mitch says, "Tickets? Anyone?"

As they walk through a basically deserted train car, we hear the Frances McDormand's recorded theme line: "Staples makes it possible."

After gaining footage and prototype visuals for these commercials, Shelly called her contact at the Staples headquarters. "In view of the fact that this is a work-from-home project, my team here at the agency wondered whether it would be more appreciated if we actually presented online. But we would also be glad to come to Framingham, Massachusetts, to present it live."

"Interesting proposition," Carol responded. "Let's see how it goes that way, but I would like to meet you."

"As would I," Shelly responded, just after a breakup with her girlfriend after a twelve-year relationship.

"As would I," Carol responded, somehow sensing the innuendo. They did.

And they did.

Shelly's Party

"**N**ext Friday will be Shelly's thirtieth birthday," Jack said matter-of-factly to his art director, Tess D'Emelia. "It's a big birthday."

"I know, and she just broke up with her girlfriend, so it might be a downer day for her."

"Should we do something special for her?" "Definitely." Tess chortled.

"She doesn't really like to be the emotional center of attention," Jack shrugged as a way to suggest that perhaps they just give her a box of chocolates or something.

"Bullshit," Tess reacted. "Everyone says that they don't want a big celebration in their honor until they get one. And then they gush. We should create a surprise party for her in conference room B. I'll handle all the decorations, balloons, napkins, cups, plates."

"You could do this?" Jack asked incredulously.

"Easy, I'll just call Party City," she scoffed. "Your dad can handle all the booze. Martin can get the finger sandwiches. Your job? Just keep her out of conference room B. Take her to lunch. Get her out of the shop. Take her to a gallery."

"Oh, I'm sure that would be just too bizarre, since we have never been to one, at least together. No, I think a lunch would be fine. I could use it as an excuse to talk about the status of the business away from the earshot of all our employees. Or maybe I could use it as an excuse for a performance review of our people."

"Well, I hope to God if I pull off this party, I would get a good performance review."

"I can guarantee it, Tess. You're the best," Jack said and gave her a hug.

Spontaneity

During the week, Tess became the "account manager" on this project. She went to the Party City in midtown and ordered a unified look for a bunch of birthday items. She picked the theme of pink and blue—not necessarily because pink was Shelly's favorite color, but because it was a thirtieth birthday, a day when people begin to feel "older." Her psychology? Those colors are throwbacks to the teenage years when everyone feels they are just a kid. Besides, she thought they were pretty.

Here's what she got for the anticipated party group of twenty people:

- Paper plates with a big *30* imprinted on it
- A tablecloth that announced "Happy 30th birthday"
- Pink plates and matching forks
- Pennant banners that announce "30-30-30"
- Cups
- Thirty lanterns to be hung from the ceiling

- Party poppers for everyone
- A birthday princess tiara
- Thirty balloons
- A pink birthday princess fedora

She arranged that the entire delivery would happen next Friday morning and be delivered to the storage room by 10:00 a.m.

Shortly after that, she spoke with Ryan O'Brien and asked him to make sure there would be enough champagne, Tito's, beer, Diet Coke, and Pellegrino water (Shelly's personal favorite). Next on her list was Martin, who was put in charge of food, desserts, and snacks. He found a caterer who could provide samosas, tiramisu, and an excellent assortment of cheeses and crackers.

The morning before, Jack had asked Shelly for a private meeting to discuss the status of the agency and perhaps the game plan for the year ahead. "Best to do this over lunch, so I made a reservation at one of my favorite restaurants in Union Square. It's called Tocqueville. Very private. Besides, it would be nice to get away from the office for a few hours. Agree?"

"I do," she said. "Should I prepare some paperwork?"

"No, let's just talk! The restaurant has an opening at 12:00 p.m., but they book up, so we shouldn't be late. OK?"

"Yes, and a good day for that," she said.

Jack and Shelly walked into Tocqueville at 12:01 p.m. and were greeted by Marco Moriera, the chef-owner. They were escorted to a private table in the main dining room. "According to my notes, you wanted some privacy," Marco asked.

"Exactly. Thanks." Jack smiled back.

Shelly looked around at the dining room. "Impressive. Is this where you take your Match.com dates?"

"Not yet, but maybe I should." He chuckled.

They both ordered a glass of Chardonnay and clinked glasses to a successful first two years in business. Shelly took a sip and then confessed, "I didn't know if this would really be successful after that first stupid Serta campaign."

"It was enough to win." Jack shrugged.

"And it has continued to be. Different is better," she admitted.

During the lunch, they saluted themselves for a string of new business success and a fair amount of positive publicity. They discussed personnel within the agency and any gaps that might need to be filled. They both felt that they had a very good staff but might need to add some backup art directors, copywriters, and perhaps a media director if they gained another client or two.

"We should be so lucky," Shelly quipped.

"We probably will," Jack confidently stated. After a pause, he added, "This feels like a wonderful, special day."

"It is," Shelly answered. "In addition to a wonderful lunch, it's my birthday."

"Nooo!" the creative director acted with perfect mock surprise. "Waiter," he called out. "Can you bring us a couple of espressos and maybe a small slice of cake, ideally with a candle?"

The restaurant obliged. Shelly blushed.

It ate up another fifteen minutes, just enough time to make sure that conference room B would be beautifully decorated for the surprise birthday party. With texts to Tessa, he was assured that everything was in place. His only text back was, "Make sure we have a camera for this."

When the two business partners walked into the agency, Naomi, the receptionist, greeted them with an ominous message: "Oh, Jack. Oh, Shelly. I am told that a very important person has been waiting in conference room B for your return. Maybe it's a new business prospect. Maybe it's a celebrity. I don't know, but I think you should head there ASAP."

Jack opened the door for Shelly to enter first and looked back at Naomi, who smiled and winked at him. *By god, with that performance, I should probably cast her in a commercial,* he thought.

When they got to conference room B, Jack asked Shelly to enter first. For a few seconds the room was dark, and then it was all lit up with pink and blue decorations, thanks to all the employees.

Immediately, they started singing, "Happy birthday to you / Happy birthday to you / Happy birthday, dear Shelly / Happy birthday to you."

Confetti was thrown. Balloons rose to the ceiling. Party poppers popped.

Ryan brought her a chair (as a throne), then a glass of champagne, and the birthday princess tiara. The camera was rolling.

Involuntarily, she started to sob out of sheer emotion. Of course, no one at the office had ever seen her break down. It was an amazing sight and a memorable moment. A hush came over the room.

"Omigod," Shelly struggled to say. "I have never been so surprised or so happy. It's all so beautiful. You are all my best friends, you really are." Tess extended one of the thirtieth-birthday napkins to Shelly to wipe away her tears. Then Shelly looked over her shoulder. "Jack, you knew about this, you schmuck. I was wondering why you were so nice to me today."

Jack just shrugged and said, "Yeah, but I didn't know it would look this pretty. Amazing. Happy birthday, my dear partner."

The party went on for a few hours. Martin's samosas and tiramisu were a hit. Ryan served as the bartender for the event and made sure everyone had at least a shot or two of

Tito's Handmade Vodka. Thanks to her new girlfriend, who attended and brought Shelly's favorite iTunes, the event even had a soundtrack other than "Happy birthday." Meanwhile, the camera continued to roll.

After about two hours, the surprise party broke up. A few employees had trains to catch and subway schedules to keep. Shelly eventually performed like a diva, moving from one group to the next, kissing everyone and thanking them for the amazing surprise. Jack O'Brien was the last one to feel her embrace. "This was wonderful," she admitted. "I don't want to cry again, but it was so special, so loving, so memorable. I don't care what everyone else says, including me: you're not really a schmuck."

"Thank you, I guess." Jack giggled and gave her a hug and waved goodbye as Shelly and her new romantic interest exited the conference room and took one last look at the aftermath of the party.

Exhausted, Tess, Jack, and his dad, Ryan, took three chairs in the midst of the debris.

"Tess, that was one of the best damn parties I have ever attended. Wow, was that emotional."

"I hate to say I told you so, but …"

"I thought the decorations were spectacular," Ryan offered.

"Beyond spectacular," Jack corrected. "Coordinated. Breathtaking. Playful. Surprising. Everything a party should be."

"I thought the booze was good," Tess congratulated the senior O'Brien as she raised her small glass of Tito's to him.

"Thank you. We didn't get rid of much wine, but the Tito's flowed." After a swig, he reflected on the evening. "She's a good woman. And she will remember this forever."

"We all will," Jack added. "But as Shelly said, 'Don't make me cry.' It was a great job. We should give each of us a raise."

"Really?" Tess asked too quickly and eagerly.

Jack had to laugh. "No, at least not on the spot but in time. You did a great job, a great job."

"I had help from Party City," Tess admitted. "They had the designs and delivered everything on time."

"Fine, but no, I go back to my initial thought. Tess, you did a great job. A great job."

After raising a congratulatory glass to each other, the three of them walked out of the agency feeling like they had indeed done a good thing.

The next week, Jack went into Tess's office and asked her to access the Party City reel, at least via YouTube. "Given your experience with them, we should pitch this account. I'll bet we could do better than anything they are running."

"Really, pitch it?" she asked. "It's basically a retail account."

"Right now it is," Jack responded. "But you proved that it's more than just paper plates, cups, and decorations. Oh. I would also like to see the videotape of the birthday celebration," he added, almost as an afterthought.

Now, to be perfectly honest, Jack O'Brien, given his position, could sometimes act as a boss. But given Tess's contribution to this event, he was determined to treat her as an equal partner. Also, in the back of his mind, he did not want to invite Shelly Lipschitz to revisit her birthday event, at least not yet.

"Let's take a look at their reel," he commanded. There were commercials for first birthdays, second birthdays, milestone birthdays, anniversaries, Christmas, Easter, Thanksgiving, Halloween, and graduation. They were basically a display of possible items for sale this weekend on each of these themes.

"This is what drives me crazy about retail advertising. It's basically a catalogue of items at price points, all of which would be better communicated in print. Why use TV to tell someone that they can buy Glad bags for $1.29?"

After a pause, Tess agreed it's a dreadful area of advertising.

After a longer pause, Jack opined, "But her surprise party was an amazing event."

"Because of the emotion," she added.

"None of which is ever captured in their advertising." "Let's look at the video tape," she suggested.

"I like the way you think."

Of course, the video was too long, but it did reveal raw emotions and a fair amount of Party City paraphernalia.

"Got an idea?" she asked.

"I do. If you can capture all the Party City shit and maybe focus on a few items—ten to twelve seconds tops—and we can focus on the emotion of the event, we can own every birthday, anniversary, graduations, and holiday, as long as we can capture the spontaneity and surprise of the moment."

"It would be like reality television in a thirty-second commercial." Tess smiled.

"Damn different." Jack high-fived her. He then took out a pen and tried to create an outline.

"It'd be interesting. I just need to make sure we have enough Party City decorations footage to make it feel colorful and festive."

"I'm sure you've got it," Jack reassured her.

"You think Shelly would agree to run it," she asked, knowing the woman's penchant for always appearing composed.

"If we make it good enough, she will. And we will," Jack reassured her.

It only took a few days to create the prototype commercial. It begins with a rough super that says, "Shelly's Surprise. Her 30th birthday party."

The door to the conference room opens. The lights go on, and balloons start to rise to the ceiling. We hear the chorus of people singing "Happy birthday party to you." We cut to Shelly, who is in sweet shock. We see Mr. O'Brien bring her a chair and place a tiara on her head. She starts to sob, and she struggles through sentences. "I have never been so surprised … or so happy." The camera then does a cinema verité scan of the birthday items—the lanterns, the plates, the napkins, the confetti, the banners. Over this we hear a voice-over give some sell copy. "Everything here came from one source. The expert in party making: Party City."

We cut back to Shelly still in her chair. Through tears, she says, "You are my best friends." Dissolve to fun in the room. A swirl of our heroine from one group to another—now laughing, hugging, kissing.

At the end, we hear a final voice-over that says, "Party City. Make someone happy." We end with Shelly leaving the room throwing a kiss to everyone as she leaves the room.

The two creative cohorts looked at the commercial in silence for a few seconds.

Finally, Tess said, "It's pretty amazing."

"And very breakthrough," Jack added. "C'mon let's show it to Shelly."

Knock, knock, knock. The two creatives entered her office and asked if she had a few minutes.

"Always for you guys," she said cheerfully.

"Did you have fun at your birthday party?" Jack asked.

She put her hand on her heart and said, "I will never forget it."

After a pause, Jack continued, "Well, just to make sure of that, we made a record of the event. You might enjoy it. Mind if I run it?"

"Be my guest."

Jack then inserted the disk and watched the emotional footage unfold.

Shelly reached for a Kleenex and relived the entire event. "Wow, it's almost like a commercial."

After a beat, Jack added, "Well, actually, it could be a commercial … with your permission."

"Omigod, most people have never seen me like that," Shelly said. "That's the beauty of it. It's real."

"It would bring out the very human side of you to all your strangers."

"I need the human side of me brought out?" she asked. Before he could offer a rebuttal, she said, "Let me see it again."

Upon review, she surprised the creative duo. "It's an astonishing thirty seconds. If it's OK with Party City, it's OK with me."

Jack immediately ejected the disk and presented it to her. "Here's a little late thirtieth-birthday present. It's an autographed copy from Tess and me. Enjoy." They then scurried out of the room rather than wait for reconsideration.

Party City loved the spot and ran it for about four months straight. Eventually, the agency created similar cinema verité spots for first birthdays, second birthdays, anniversaries, and graduations.

Perhaps you have seen them all. If not, you should go to Party City and just create an event of your own. Surprise someone. And as the commercials say in the last line, "Make someone happy."

The First Defection

Martin walked into Shelly's office quite sheepishly. "Shelly, I have been offered another job, and I think I should take it."

She held up a finger to shush him and speed-dialed her secretary. "Rose, can you get Jack here in my office immediately? It's urgent."

Within a minute, Jack slid into her office like Michael Richards in *Friends*. "Yo, what's up?"

Shelly asked the impulsive creative director to take a seat. "Our expert planner, Martin, here is tempted to jump ship and take a different job."

"You can't," Jack immediately objected. "You are critical to this place. And you single-handedly inspired the M&M's campaign. So just get that thought out of your mind."

After a pause, Martin answered, "I can't. I love this place, and everyone here makes me feel like family. But I miss my country, and my previous employer wants me back, with a fairly generous raise."

"Yeah, but will it be as fun?" Jack rebutted, pulling at straws.

"Probably not, but perhaps I've had enough fun in the past few years to last me for a while."

"And we can offer you a fairly generous raise," Shelly offered. Martin just shook his head. "Shelly, it's not really about the money."

There were a few seconds of silence while everyone gathered his or her thoughts and best arguments.

Jack held up his hands as if asking for a prayer. "Martin, Shelly and I had lunch a few days ago, and we were trying to take a good, hard look at the quality of our staff. We agreed that we have the best employees in the business, especially for a small shop. And you are critical to that." Martin just shrugged.

"What's the agency that's trying to woo you?" Shelly asked. "BBH. I worked there before."

"So it would be the same old, same old."

"Have you already accepted the job?" Jack asked. "No, not yet," Martin lied.

"OK, so I want you to think about this for a few days. Take a few days off, see this wonderful city. Fall in love again with Manhattan. Meanwhile, Shelly and I will try to figure out if there's anything we can do to change your mind."

"Thank you," Martin said and exited the room.

"Any chance he stays?" Shelly asked.

"I doubt it. It sounds like his mind in made up. We should probably come up with a new compensation package for him, but it seems to me that he really wants to return to the UK."

"Maybe he misses his brothers and sisters and cousins," she added.

"Who knows? But I think we should alert a recruiter just to see if there is another strategic planner that might be interested in joining the hottest creative shop in Manhattan."

Two days later, Martin reentered Shelly's office. As soon as he did, she called Jack. "We may have a verdict here on dear Martin."

The two partners sat around the cocktail table, and Martin took a deep breath. "I have thought about it and thought about it and thought about it," he said. "I really think I should go back to London. It's my roots. It's where my family is. And I know the job."

"We have reassessed your salary here," Shelly feebly offered.

Before she could say much more, he held up his hand. "I appreciate that, but it's not about the money."

"I understand."

"Well, you have made amazing contributions here, and you will be missed. How many more days or weeks do we have with you?"

"Two weeks' notice. Isn't that customary in the USA?"

"Indeed it is," Jack responded. "Martin, I want you to take one of these M&M's prints as a memento of the impact you made here. And we wish you all the best."

With that, both Shelly and Jack rose from their chairs and gave him a hearty handshake.

After a few seconds, both lifted their hands up in a "What else could we do?" gesture.

"Any luck on new strategic planner replacements?" Jack asked. "Got a few good prospects," she admitted.

"I tend to prefer the Brit planners. I think they just sound smarter to most clients."

"Agree. Central casting. Two are Brits who have lived in the US for several years, so they are probably not homesick."

"Onward and upward," Jack said and returned to his daily schedule of creative reviews.

Drugs—They're Not As Good As You Thought

Given their reputation for breakthrough creative work and the recent headlines about their "ingenious solutions" in the advertising press, it was not surprising that they were approached by the Partnership for Drug-Free Kids to do a pro bono spot for the organization. That's basically the way it works with this prestigious organization. They reach out to the most amazing (and sometimes most revered) ad agencies in town for the privilege of creating meaningful advertising to save kids from drugs. They can sometimes be partially reimbursed for production expenses. But as for creative expenses? That's a contribution.

The ground rules were as follows:

The agency must be quite creatively sensitive and rather willing to embrace courageous creative work.

It's usually a one-time commitment, so the financial exposure is very limited. The Partnership sets the strategy. While it is somewhat negotiable, it saves the agency the agita of discovering the ins, the outs, and the in-betweens of kids getting addicted to drugs.

In this case, the strategy was called Think Twice. The theory was, everyone is tempted. Once may be one time too many. Obviously, there was a full sheet of strategy and back up, but that's the gist.

In preparation, Jack asked a new, young team at the agency if they wanted to take a crack at it. "I don't know. I use drugs occasionally, and I like it," the copywriter said.

"I use pot quite a bit," the art director answered. "Helps loosen my mind."

"Too much information," Jack replied. "Let me think about this."

Purely out of curiosity (and because he no longer had a strategic planner in house), he wondered if this was typical in the agency. So he drafted an email to the entire staff:

We are planning to create a breakthrough commercial for the Partnership for Drug-Free Kids. But to prepare, I need more information from the staff. This will be completely confidential. Just answer the following three questions, run off a copy, and place it in the box by the receptionist. Totally confidential. Do not even write in the answers (I don't want to identify anyone's penmanship). This can help us deliver an award-winning commercial.

Question 1: Have you ever used illegal drugs?

Question 2: What did you think when you first indulged? In other words, why? Thrills? Experimentation? Escape?

Question 3: Please identify any negative effect that you or your friends may have experienced as a result, i.e., jail time, death, and homelessness. Success? You name it.

Again, don't sign this. I just want some information and insights from folks who may be younger than me.

He had a hunch that at least 60 percent of his staff still used drugs. It almost pushed him to call the Partnership for Drug-Free Kids and recuse himself from this assignment.

"Did you fill out your form?" Shelly asked, entering his office. "Yes," Jack answered.

"Well, I will tell you how I filled out my form," she asserted.

"I don't want to know. I don't want to know," Jack answered, covering his ears.

"And you?"

"You don't want to know. You don't want to know." He sighed.

"That's the problem," Shelly advised. "No one wants to talk about it. This might be your first yakety-yak-yak commercial," she added and exited his office.

After a few moments, he relooked at the confidential statements and then crafted a revelatory commercial about misperceptions of drug thrills.

With Tess's help, they reached out through *Backstage* to find actors who would be willing to play drug-addicted citizens, with the following promises: You will not be identified. In fact, you will be intentionally blurred. Also, your voice will be distorted, so it will not impede your ability to get a role in *Hamilton*. Scale only … but an easy two-to-three-hour shoot."

Not surprisingly, they had 120 actors in the agency lobby at 9:00 a.m. By 2:00 p.m., Tess and Jack had casted the commercial. By noon the next morning, they had edited the masterpiece.

To be honest, it was sort of a weird commercial. What else would you expect from O'Brien, Lipschitz, and Partners?

The Spot

The drama begins with three supers that descend on each other. They say,
    I thought.
    I thought.
    I thought.
A new super appears: Real people. Real thoughts.
The camera reveals a blurry young man with a disguised voice:
Man 1: I thought it would give me an escape from my ugly reality.
Woman 2: I thought it would unleash my creativity.
Young man: I thought it might make me more acceptable as a gay American.
Young man: I thought it might make me funnier.
Young woman: I thought it might make me sexier.

The scene dissolves to a table shot of cocaine, needles, and pot, all of which magically blows away over the super "And then what happened?"

Man 1: My best friend overdosed and is now dead.

Young man: Nothing happened—as in nothing to do, nowhere to go, no one to see.

Woman 2: I found it more difficult to create. Now I serve coffee.

Young man: Instead of being funnier, I was angrier.

Young man: My gay friends don't care. As a matter of fact, they would like me more aware.

Young man: I thought it would be better.

Woman: I thought it would be cooler.

Teenager: I thought it would be more exciting.

Final super: Drugs—they're not as good as you thought.

Become More Delicious

The agency's new strategic planner, a British woman named Meryl Shimkus (who had come from Ogilvy & Mather), was something of a gung ho cheerleader. "Work should be fun," she told Jack in her first interview.

"Yeah, and it is," he responded.

"Well, maybe it should be even more fun." she retorted.

Shelly had known her from her previous agency and had convinced Jack that she could be an infusion of a new spirit. "High-energy girl," she said.

"I've noticed."

"She wants to organize a team cooking class at Sur La Table for all the employees."

"Are you fucking kidding me? I can't even boil an egg," Jack scoffed. "And it's bullshit team building. Team building is working on an advertising project and winning it. Have you ever done such a cooking thing before?"

Shelly smiled. "I have. It's actually kind of fun. Everybody gets put into teams of three of four people. Everyone divides task. Some get the ingredients. Some cut. Some stir. At the end, we all eat together and enjoy a few drinks."

"What's the cuisine?"

"Soups."

Jack just sighed. "Well, that doesn't sound too hard. You just open up the can and heat it up, right?"

Shelly just shook her head. "Jack, sometimes you are hopeless, but almost always funny."

The entire staff gathered on the following Wednesday at Sur La Table on West Fifty-Sixth. The chef, a sparkling young woman named Sabrina Johnson, introduced her staff for the evening. They included Robert—her assistant—and Juan, who would be handling all the dishwashing. She then passed around a portfolio of ten recipes and asked the group to introduce themselves.

"My name is Meryl Shimkus, and I sort of wanted all our employees to share this as a team-building exercise. We all work together."

Almost immediately, Jack O'Brien stood up rather than cede the floor. "I'm Jack O'Brien, the creative director of O'Brien, Lipschitz, and Partners—the hottest ad agency in New York and maybe in America. We're here to cook together but also to ascertain whether this might be a good new business prospect for us."

"Wow!" Sabrina exclaimed. "Hey, crew, we better be on our best behavior. We may end up being on television."

After a chuckle, the rest of the staff introduced themselves to Sabrina, who then outlined the recipes and explained that there were a few tricky spots like roasting the chicken and sautéing the butternut squash. She preliminarily performed a demo for these procedures.

She then delineated the recipes:

- Tomato-basil soup
- French onion
- Baked potato soup
- Butternut-squash soup
- Broccoli cheese
- Clam chowder
- Chicken and fried rice
- Roasted-chicken noodle
- Vietnamese pho
- And two dessert soups:
    - Watermelon gazpacho
    - Peach ginger soup

By counting 1-2-3-4, she created four groups of four different recipe groups. Jack was fortunately teamed with Tess and, as luck would have it, with Meryl the Cheerleader. Fortunately, his dad Ryan was also in his group, and the creative director hoped that his dad's acerbic wit could somehow curb the rah-rah of Ms. Shimkus.

Group 1 was given the following assignments: Butternut squash soup, broccoli cheese, baked potato soup, and watermelon gazpacho dessert soup.

As instructed, the group divided chores: Ryan gathered a lot of the ingredients. Tess wrapped the potatoes and put them in the oven. Meryl cut the butternut squash into pieces and sautéed them. Jack cut the watermelon.

Meanwhile, the group compared notes about their respective progress.

"I think we are already ahead of the other groups," Meryl remarked with a positive clinched fist.

"Is it a race?" Ryan O'Brien asked sarcastically.

"No, but if you fall behind, you get sloppy," Meryl answered as she continued to dice the butternut squash.

"So true," Jack acerbically added and continued to cut the watermelon into cubes while saving a few beautiful slices.

The actual recipes were not particularly difficult. The roasted-chicken noodle soup was a bit challenging. So was the clam chowder, since someone had to secure the clam meat from the shells. The fried rice took a little finesse but was a rather quick process.

Of course, Sabrina, the chef, visited every group to make sure there were no snafus. At 8:00 p.m., she also announced it would be thirty minutes to service time. "Everything that needs to be cooked should be on the stove by now. At 8:30, we sit down and share!"

To Jack's surprise, he actually enjoyed the experience. He even found a common ground with his new strategic planner, Meryl Shimkus. At one point, she fell behind, and sensing that Jack was ahead of schedule, she asked if he could possibly keep an eye on the noodles "so they don't get too, too soft."

"I hate soft, soft noodles," he agreed and knew the al dente taste test from meals in Italian restaurants.

At 8:20 p.m., Sabrina invited all participants to plate their food. For his gazpacho soup, Jack asked his favorite art director, Tess D'Emelia, to give a little extra oomph to his gazpacho soup. She created a tour de force. The soup was placed as a centerpiece, surrounded by luscious pieces of California watermelon.

Everyone oohed and partook of the dessert offering. Even Sabrina, the chef, remarked that it was one of their prettiest dishes. "Maybe you should be our ad agency," she quipped. "Can we get a picture?" Of course the cameras came out, and there were records of every soup created, most of which Jack had to admit were great.

Along with wine, it was a successful evening. Within a week, the watermelon gazpacho soup was on the website.

Within six weeks (with some urging from Chef Sabrina, who called it a particularly encouraging and fun group), the ad agency was contacted by Sur La Table in Seattle to ascertain if they would be interested in talking about handing their advertising campaign.

The ad director, a certain Michelle Carlyle, admitted that she had looked at the agency's website and was impressed. Thanks to the agency's contact numbers, he reached Shelly Lipschitz and asked if the agency might be interested in handling their cooking class advertising. "We already have an agency for our retail goods, but the fastest-growing part of our business is the cooking classes."

"That would be the most interesting part of the business to us," Shelly admitted.

"I see that one of your employees, a woman named Meryl Shimkus, has been to several of our classes, and we are thankful for that. But most of you were first timers. I trust you enjoyed the experience?"

"We loved it," Shelly answered. "And we would love to encourage more people to enjoy the experience."

"Great. Let's exchange contact numbers and figure out a rough timetable when you could come to Seattle and share your thoughts."

Within four weeks, Jack, Shelly, Tess, and Meryl were in Seattle to present a spiffy cooking campaign for Sur La Table.

Thanks to Meryl's focus groups, she discovered that it wasn't all about the finished product. To her surprise, it was not all about teamwork—although that was much appreciated by all the participants. It was basically about the growth—the chance to challenge yourself with your head, your hands, and your heart to create something new beyond college.

As a matter of fact, Jack did want to try out the line in one of the research groups. It resonated with many but also came off as too methodical. No, what was required was something more emotional.

Actually, Meryl suggested a line. "What if we promised that you could become more successful, more accomplished, more desirable. How about 'Become more delicious'?"

Jack laughed out loud and bowed. "I love that line. Wow. This may be perfect teamwork after all."

In the next week, Tess and Jack created several commercials of working people taking the Sur La Table classes. In one, a middle-aged woman learned tiramisu and brought the finished product back to her husband, who danced her into the bedroom. In another, a young man surprised his young love with class-baked French macaroons. They began feeding each other until the screen went dark with the lines "Sur La Table. Become more delicious."

Michelle, the client, grinned at each execution. "I do love them, but do you think we could include a website at the end so people would know which particular classes are available in their hometown?"

"Oh, I don't know that that's possible," Jack remarked with a mock saddened face. "It might ruin the integrity of the creative product." After a beat, he looked at Meryl, slapped his knee, and guffawed. "Of course, we can do that! It could help build enrollment and make the brand even more successful."

Done. Within a few months, the commercials were on the air, and many more people were becoming more delicious.

Shouldn't Your Dog
Eat Better than You?

Tess bounced into the office on this particular Monday, beaming with pride and photos. She showed them to Jack, who remarked, "They don't look like you."

"Of course not. It's my new dog. Got it yesterday. It's a Yorkie mutt that just wants to lick my face."

"Aw, c'mon. Don't talk nasty to me," Jack teased. "Did you pay thousands of dollars for this exotic breed?"

"Actually, she was a shelter dog. When I went there and they let her out of her cage, she jumped up, asking to be held and immediately licked my face. I would say it was love at first lick."

"Again, don't talk nasty to me," he teased. "What's her name?" "Whitney."

"After the Whitney Museum?"

"No, after Whitney Miller, who was Miss United States in 2012 and a professional wake surfer on a journey to win a jujitsu black belt. I like the combination of beauty and healthy." Tess bragged about her name research.

"Got a picture?"

Tess again extended a picture of her new pet.

"No, I want to see Miss USA in 2012 with the great athletic body." "Google it," Tess advised. "Anyway, I want Whitney to be super healthy, so I asked the vet at the shelter what I should feed her. He recommended," she looked at her notes, "Wellness CORE dog food. It has above-average protein, near-average fat, and below-average carbs. Most importantly, I looked them up, and they do *not* have an existing ad agency, but they have many products at Walmart, Amazon, and other online companies. Google it, after you get a good look at the real Whitney Miller. If you would like, I could bring cute little Whitney into work tomorrow so you could meet my dear dog."

"No, no, no, no pets," Jack protested. "If I have to, I will issue a memo saying no dogs, cats, gerbils, snakes, or ferrets allowed in the shop."

"Fair enough," Tess said. "But I hope we can find a way to keep my dear Whitney healthy."

After his favorite art director left his office, he did go on Google. Truth be told, he did access pictures and a bio of Whitney Miller. Wow! After that visual, he tried to apply it to the dog photo he had on his desk. Then he accessed Wellness CORE dog food. While he was in no way a health freak, he was impressed by the credentials of the brand.

The basic recipe contained chicken, chicken meal, turkey meal, potato, peas, and tomato. Other varieties included salmon, wild game, beef, boar, lamb, and other goodies. All were natural, quality ingredients.

Jack did a head jolt. "By god, this is a better diet than any of my friends have. What, no quarter pounders? What, no mac and cheese? What, no strawberry cheesecake?"

The next morning, he proposed a campaign to his amazing art director. "Do you exercise your new dog?"

"Every morning," she responded. "I want her to be healthy." "And you want to feed her just as well?"

"Of course."

"I think it's impressive," Jack acknowledged. "And I would like to recommend a campaign on fitness, diet, and health."

"I would just say, look at the Rachel Ray campaign for Nutrish," she cautioned him. "People like it, and it's about a good diet for your dog."

"Yeah, but she looks fat. You don't. Would you give me the permission to put you in a dog food commercial for Whitney?"

"Yes."

"In a leotard … with your dear dog?" After a pause, she agreed.

It was the first commercial O'Brien, Lipschitz, and Partner ever shot with special effects.

Visually, it begins with the instructor who is strangely robed in a veterinarian outfit from behind. He turns around and reveals an open robe with squeezer swimming briefs and addresses his class, "OK, today we are going to get very, very healthy. Let's start with the exercise. Stretch. Stretch. Stretch."

We cut to the class and see Tess D'Emelia stretching her legs to her left and right. We also see her pet, Whitney, doing the same exact thing. As we pan, we see several other dogs equally exercising, thanks to special effects.

The dogs are doing the same sort of exercises you do in the gym, in perfect timing with each other. The dogs are of all breeds—German shepherds, golden retrievers, dalmatians, pugs, poodles, you name it. They were there, doing their exercises in perfect, surreal harmony.

Cut to the instructor. "OK, on your stomachs. Stretch your right leg then your left." All the dogs do this. So does Tess.

"Pushups!" the instructor screams. Everyone turns over. Tess does a few.

Thanks to special effect, so do the various dogs.

"But it's not all about exercise. It's also about diet," the vet/coach instructs. "And we have Wellness CORE here in the corner to keep you amazingly healthy. Who's hungry?"

All the dogs race to the bowls of dog food with packages for branding.

The vet/coach approaches Tess and comments, "You're doing a good thing for your dog."

"OK, but where's the nearest junk food place for me?"

"Really?"

Cut to all the dogs eating healthily with branding packages of Wellness CORE. All the dogs are scarfing it up.

Over this final visual, they super the brand and a line: "Wellness CORE Dog Food. Shouldn't your dog eat better than you?"

As a button, Tess asks the vet/coach, "You say it's three blocks away?"

"Maybe four."

The title again shows: "Shouldn't your dog eat better than you?"

When they arrived at their apartment, Whitney bounded up to the second- floor apartment. Immediately, Tess made some macaroni and cheese for herself and then poured a bowl of Wellness CORE dog food for her new best friend, Whitney. As she stirred her own lunch meal, she offered it to the dog. "Want some mac 'n' cheese?"

Similar to the CGI special effect in the aforementioned commercial, the dog shook her head no in real time and then returned to her bowl of Wellness CORE.

Ironic proof: When you are on the way to health, temptations don't quite work.

DIY

Shelly Lipchitz brought the gadget into the office on this bright spring morning after her Passover holiday. "I met this guy at the high holy days. His name is Daniel Birnbaum, and he was visiting from Israel. He's the CEO of this gizmo, which could be an amazing success in the US."

"What is it?" Jack asked.

"Soda Stream," Shelly answered as if she were an oracle of the obvious. "With it, you can make any number of carbonated beverages—such as cola, Fanta, Crystal Lite, Country Time, Ocean Spray, Root Beer, diet drinks, iced tea. You name it, it can make it. Less bottles and cans in the fridge. Less in the trash. Fresher taste."

She then showed the CO_2 cartridge. "It's basically carbonated water with great flavors. I told him we should do their advertising."

"Where are they located?"

"Forty-one countries, with headquarters in Lod, Israel. Ever been?"

"I've been to Ireland," Jack retorted. "Is that close?"

"Not very, but Israel is fun."

"So's Ireland."

"C'mon, what kind of flavor would you like?"

"Nah, I've got some cans of ginger ale in the fridge."

"Save the cans," Shelly admonished. "I'll make you a ginger ale from scratch."

She then searched for the right flavor package, the CO_2 cartridge, and a pitcher of water and plugged in the device.

Within a matter of minutes, she had a quart of freshly made ginger ale. She poured a glass for Jack, who looked skeptically at it but then took a sip. He smiled.

"Not bad," he admitted.

"Better than not bad," Shelly corrected him. "Better than Canada Dry."

"Is it a successful business?"

"Twenty percent of all homes in Sweden use this. Imagine if we had a 20 percent penetration in the US. We'd be bigger than the Coke brand."

Jack took another sip. "I like it," he said. "Let's win it."

In preparation, Jack looked at their reel of existing commercials. There was one he particularly admired. It showed a bunch of railroad car containers of empty crushed soda cans. The message: "This is the amount of trash you could save in one year if you switched from canned soda to Soda Stream." It was dramatic. It was impressive. And it had a great theme line: "If you love the bubbles, set them free."

"Wow!" Jack exclaimed, rarely raving about a competitive agency's commercials. "What's the matter with that commercial?"

"They couldn't run it on the Super Bowl. Coke and Pepsi complained that it was disparaging. And as two of the biggest Super Bowl advertising, they prevailed."

"It's an eco message and a damn good one, but if you can't get it on the air, what's the point?" Shelly argued. "Besides, the client would rather compliment the flavor and the ease of operation. They don't want to get shut out again from major advertising venues."

"Shit, that's a damn good commercial, and it's young oriented."

"You can do better," Shelly encouraged him.

Meryl ran many focus groups to try to find a point of difference. With Shelly's help, they made instant cola, sparkling lemonade, and diet ginger ale (made with Splenda). They ran groups of teens, twentysomethings, and middle-aged parents.

In every case, the product was a hit. It did taste good and freshly carbonated.

Meryl probed different strategic advantages. Taste ended up being a slight advantage. It was good, but not measurably better than an eight-ounce bottle of Coca-Cola classic. Hey, how good is that, especially with all those memories?

The convenience factor was a plus, since you could make six or seven different flavors without visiting the grocery store six or seven times.

The biggest emotion came from comparing this homemade drink to the conglomerate offerings of big business. Perhaps this was a holdover from the Trump, anti-big persecution complex that had begun to afflict middle-class America.

Without much provocation, the group got off the Soda Stream product and began to rail against imported cars, global business, and the crush of small shops everywhere.

"So is this a small business?" Meryl innocently asked. "It's the smallest of businesses. You make it yourself."

"I love that. You don't have to make the fat cats fatter," one middle-class white male summed it up.

After another twenty minutes of complaints against the big "tax break guys," Meryl entered the back room behind the one-way mirror and held up her hands.

Jack volunteered the first reaction, "It's ugly out there."

Meryl agreed but said, "Yes, but it's real, and the chance to buck big business may prove the most leverageable advantage we can find."

"OK, but beyond the anger and disenfranchisement that so many feel, is there a positive emotion in that?"

Without hesitation, Meryl answered, "Yes, it's the American sense of being independent, self-made, self-done. It existed in every age group."

Semi-encouraged, he asked Meryl to please issue a two-page summary of her last comments.

With Tess's help and thanks to stock footage, they created a visual anthem of mass production. Smokestacks. Packets. Soft drinks on the assembly line.

(Given the recent litigation, they were careful to not identify Coke or Pepsi. For all we knew from the footage, it could have beer or water—no labels. The point of the footage was mass production.)

Music creates a boredom beat.

The voice-over says, "It's made a thousand bottles an hour and a million dollars a day. And in the end, we all pay."

The bottles on the assembly line begin to speed up. And when they do, they begin the blur.

We cut to the gadget.

"There is a wonderful, enlightened alternative. One hundred flavors. Two and a half minutes per quart. Ultimate satisfaction. Taste."

Cut to a kid enjoying a glass with his mom. Rather than saying "Wow, Mom, that's great," the kid gives her a hug.

Just to break the Pollyanna nature of this commercial, a blank page appears and a hand-stitched logo begins to appear. Stitch after stitch, ultimately, it spells out the words "DIY. Soda Stream."

The voice-over explains the abbreviations: "Do it yourself. Soda Stream."

The Best Small Agency
of the Year

Once a year, *Adweek* does their rankings of ad agencies. Often the big agencies enjoy repeat accolades—Ogilvy & Mather, McCann-Erickson, Young & Rubicam.

The smaller agencies are inevitably more competitive. An odd campaign can push one upstart agency into the top ten. A strange ad can catapult a Soho agency into monthly fame. But to be dubbed the best, an agency must show a sustained array of break-through advertising over the past twelve months.

O'Brien, Lipschitz, and Partners won the award this year—mostly on the basis of a sustained effort to break barriers and amuse people with their irreverent work. Dave's Day, a strange celebration of Dave Thomas's death on behalf of Wendy's, was paramount. Other accolades went to their work for Party City ("Make someone happy"), Tito's ("The handmade cowboy vodka"), and their brand-new campaign for Sur La Table ("Become more delicious").

According to Joel Crawford, who wrote the piece, "The agency rarely takes the easy, expected path. Lots of their work is absurd, and I mean that in a good way.

"Often the commercials are quite funny. The spots rarely catalogue every item in a retail store. They prefer to tell a human story. As their agency motto says, 'the truth … with a twist.'"

The article featured some key frames from their commercials and several of their better print ads. It also included an interview with Shelly and Jack.

Interviewer: In your opinion, what makes your agency special?

Shelly: I would say the people. We have a very good staff of imaginative young people.

Jack: I would also say that we have an attitude to challenge the status quo. Yeah, a big part of that comes from a young workforce, but the mood has to be set from management.

Interviewer: How do you do that?

Jack: Like a lot of agencies, we use research. But we use it in a different way than other places. We rarely test our finished ideas. Instead, we use focus groups to plum the emotions of the consumers we are trying to reach.

Shelly: As a matter of fact, we just hired a new strategic planner—Meryl Shimkus. She's excellent at unearthing people's inner moods and attitudes.

Interviewer: So a lot of your commercials do not endure the rigors of day- after recall?

Shelly: Most of them don't.

Interviewer: How do you manage that? Don't a lot of clients require it?

Shelly: Mostly the big-package clients.

Jack: I guess we have a different caliber of client. Maybe a little more adventurous. I think we do a good job selling the idea and the emotional connection to the brand.

Interviewer: How many employees do you have?

Shelly: Twenty-one and counting.

Interviewer: Who is your head art director? I think the work has a very good look.

Jack: Her name is Tess D'Emelia. She's young but has a great design sense. I usually work directly with her as a creative team. She has a great attitude.

Interviewer: Have you pitched and lost accounts?

(There was a pause. Shelly and Jack looked at each to jog their memories.)

Shelly: I don't think so.

Jack: No.

Interviewer: Wow, what a track record. You really do deserve to be the small agency of the year. Shelly, incidentally, I saw you in that Party City commercial. You could have a second career as an actress.

Shelly: Well, I wasn't acting. I was just overcome with emotion. It was a surprise party. And this goof (*pointing to Jack*) took me to a long lunch so the room could be decorated. Total surprise.

Interviewer: Very nice spot. "Make someone happy." So what's ahead for O'Brien, Lipschitz, and Partners?

Shelly: Onward and upward.

Interviewer: Do you envision doubling the size of the agency in the next year?

Jack: Oh, I hope not. I love this size agency.

Interviewer: Well, congratulations again. I wonder if we can get a few extra pictures of the two of you standing together in front of your sign at the front desk.

Shelly: Gladly.

The photographer took seven or eight shots. The *Adweek* personnel and the agency principals shook hands.

When they exited, the duo looked at each other. Jack said, "I thought we did pretty well."

Shelly replied, "Absolutely, we said all the right things. Even made sure we mentioned some of our key players so it wasn't all about us."

"We may end up getting more new business out of this."

"I wouldn't be surprised."

Once the feature story hit in *Adweek*, it did create a buzz in the industry. Jack and Shelly got several congratulatory calls from their friends in the industry. Many of the employees were similarly feted by their friends.

At least in the initial days after the story was published, they did not get calls from new business prospects. However, they did get dozens of calls from advertising folks at competing agencies who expressed an interest in joining the hot firm.

"We don't need to hire anyone right now," Jack admitted.

"No, but we should probably look at all their résumés and perhaps even have a few interviews, just in case we do gain another account or two."

"We could probably use a head of production," Jack said.

"I'll go over the stack of CVs and see if anyone qualifies." Shelly retorted.

"I just don't want to get too big," Jack reiterated.

Shelly reassured him, "It took us this long to get this big. It could take us years to double our size."

"Or we could just pitch and lose a few."

"Ha, ha, ha," Shelly gave a mock laugh. "That's not in our DNA."

"No, it isn't," Jack O'Brien agreed.

Readers Cheaters

Within a month, O'Brien, Lipschitz, and Partners was invited to pitch three different accounts—Readers online glasses, Grubhub, and Kumon math and reading help for kids three-plus.

All presentations were due at the same time, about five weeks from now. That would create a miserable traffic jam of creative work, and every presentation would inevitably suffer.

Given the fact that none of the employees had young children, Shelly and Jack wisely decided to pass on Kumon. It was too alien for the staff. Also, as Jack opined, it would probably end up with "cute" advertising—not their forte.

Grubhub was tempting from a hip standpoint, but Shelly rightly assessed that they already had too many food/restaurant products—namely Hooters and Wendy's. This, she predicted, would be the straw that broke both camels' back.

There were a few people in the agency that used reading glasses. Jack's dad, Ryan, had worn them for decades. (Actually, he had recently changed to bifocals.) Shelly had just started wearing reading glasses last year. Jack started wearing them (with a very low magnification) a few months ago. He felt it was getting more difficult to read the fine print in the phone book and simply went to CVS to buy a cheap pair. Ironically, he loved the look. "Makes me look smart," he told Tess. "Don't you think?"

"Einstein," she retorted. "OK, maybe not that smart."

They looked on the website and saw hundreds of choices, most of which were under thirty dollars. Jack was like a kid in a toy store. He kept pointing to glasses and asked his art director. "Does this one make me look even smarter? How about this one? Ooh, ooh, sort of Ben Franklin glasses. Wow, that is smart!"

"You're already smart enough," Tess answered.

Jack bowed and blew a kiss to his art director, as if she were a performer at Carnegie Hall. "Thank you. Thank you very much."

"Who's the competition?" Tess asked.

Shelly had just entered the room and answered, "Every single drugstore. Online, their only real competition is Eye Bobs. Not bad. A little more expensive but a little nerdier."

"What do they want from an ad campaign?" Jack asked.

"All we need to do is draw people to the Reader's website. Once someone is on it, they tend to buy three to four glasses."

"This is a layup." Jack high-fived the group.

"Not so fast, Kowalski," Shelly warned with a schoolyard chant. "They already have an agency called the Concept Farm. They tend to do a pretty good job. Part of me thinks all they want to do is shake it up with them so the agency doesn't take the account for granted."

"Ugly," Jack reacted. "Is the work any good?"

"It's not bad. They show ten people of all different types—teachers, business folk, secretaries, lawyers, eggheads, construction guys looking at blueprints, etc., etc.—with the promise that Readers can match your unique personality."

"So another catalogue on the airwaves." Jack blew a breath of frustration at the predictability of the agency business. "Let's get Meryl to run some groups. I want twenty glasses on the table. I want to know how people *feel* when they put one on the tip of their noses."

What Meryl discovered was something that Jack instinctively knew: People feel smarter wearing these reading glasses. They feel more respected. They feel more scholarly and better read. It flatters their ego and their self-concept. It didn't take long for Tess and Jack to create a wonderful campaign. The theme line was utter simplicity: "Readers. Look smart."

The commercial was a slice of life. In it, a thirtysomething man is showing an architectural plan to a group of clients. He is having difficulty keeping their attention. "I'm sorry, what were you saying?" one client asks the man. As he tries to continue, another client asks his buddy, who is getting up from the table, "Hey, can you get me a cup of coffee?" It's chaos in this meeting room.

"Let's take a closer look at the blueprint," our hero says and puts on a pair of light-brown Readers. "I see a large open atrium here"—the architect points to the center of the blueprint—"and individual office surrounding the green space."

Two clients look at each other and nod.

"I think that's brilliant," one says.

"Clever. Very clever." The other client gestures with a thumbs-up.

A voice-over says, "When you're wearing Readers, it's easy to see what a difference it makes."

The camera then shows several different Readers in various colors for about five to six seconds.

"And it clearly gives you an advantage in any situation."

Our hero architect, wearing his Readers, again points to the blueprint.

Architect: Now I think all of you in this room should have the biggest offices around the atrium.

A client: This guy is so, so bright.

Another client: Intuitive.

Another client: Dazzling.

Another client: Brilliant.

Voice-over: Readers.com. Look smart.

Shelly, Tess, Meryl, and Jack loved the spot and presented it with gusto at their new business presentation. To be honest, the clients seemed to like the insight and enjoy the commercial.

"We're just trying to get people to think of Readers not just as a prescriptive medical need but also as a badge of intelligence," Jack gave his closing argument. "You, who buy Readers, know enough to demand the very best, to put your best foot forward, and to carry the day." He then put on his newly purchased Readers and summed up his pitch. "At least that's how I feel when I look smart."

Around the conference table, the clients smiled and seemed to appreciate the effort and the angle.

"Excellent job," the head client said. "We'll get back to you in a few days."

Within forty-eight hours, the client called Shelly and announced that Readers had decided to stay with their existing agency.

"Wow, we are not used to losing," she admitted. "What tipped the scales?"

"First of all, let me say that we thought you guys did a great job," the client said. Blah, blah, blah. "But we know the Concept Farm and thought they did an outstanding job for our needs."

"Such as?"

"They showed ten or fifteen different people with ten or fifteen different Readers with the line 'Looks like you.'"

"So sort of a catalogue of a lot of your products with a lot of different-type people?"

"Exactly!"

"Well, obviously we are disappointed, but we wish you the best. And thank you for the opportunity."

"It was our pleasure to meet your team. Very impressive," the client said and hung up.

Shelly took a deep breath and then waited a few minutes before going into Jack's office. "We didn't get it," she said. "They decided to stay in their comfort zone with their existing agency."

"No!" Jack exclaimed. "Yes," Shelly answered.

"What's the campaign?"

"Looks like you." Fifteen different people. Fifteen different glasses."

"Give me a fucking break. If you've got brown hair, we have brown glasses. If you have gray hair, we have gray glasses. Red hair, red glasses. Please!" Jack exclaimed with exasperation. "You predicted this," he told Shelly. "You had this hunch that maybe they just wanted to send a wake-up call to their present agency. Schmucks!"

"I should probably send a nice email and thank-you to all the staff that worked so hard on the pitch," she suggested.

"Yeah," he nodded. "Well, I guess there is always a first time." "Just not meant to be."

"Schmucks," he repeated. He shook his head and exited the office.

Love Beats Money

Even though his door was always open, there was knock on it, and a rather sheepish Shelly Lipschitz was standing in the doorway.

"Jack, I need to have a serious talk with you," she said.

"What did I do now?" he asked jokingly.

"Nothing, you're good. But I do need to talk with you."

"Talk away."

Shelly took a deep breath and then began. "Remember that article when we were named the best small agency of the year?"

"I've already had it laminated," he kidded her.

"Yeah, and remember when we had a few dozen applicants wanting to join this wonderful agency?"

"Yep, and I already met with the guy who wants to be head of production, good meeting," the creative director answered, anticipating her question.

"It's not about that," she corrected him. "On the basis of that glowing article, I got a call from BBDO, and they would like me to join as head of account management."

Jack pushed his chair back in stunned silence. "That's impossible."

Shelly struggled with her answer. "No, it's actually quite possible. The CEO knew me from my days at Ogilvy, and when he read the article in *Adweek*, he told me that he thought I was probably better than ever and could most likely bring some needed spunk to BBDO."

"We lose one pitch out of eighteen months, and you're ready to walk out the door," he criticized.

"It's not about the Readers pitch. The work was great. They just wanted to send a scare to their existing agency. I told you that."

"Yes, you did."

They both just stared at each other for several seconds, then Shelly continued. "They want to give me half the agency to manage and put me on the board of directors."

"You already have half the agency to manage, and you're already on the board of directors, which is basically you and me."

"Jack, don't make this more difficult than it already is. They offered me twice the salary I get here at O'Brien, Lipschitz, and Partners."

"Yeah, but will they change the name of the agency to BBDO Lipschitz?"

"You know, Jack, you are a card."

Jack let this all sink in and was puzzled as to how to address the money issue. Given their finances, he could not double her salary, but he had a hope he could somehow address the disparity. "When are you supposed to meet with this asshole CEO at BBDO Lipschitz? I am sorry, wrong name of the agency. Of course, your name is not on the door. When?"

"Tomorrow morning," she answered.

"Don't jump," he cautioned her. "Think of all you have here. Think of all we have built. Think of the future we can have."

"I think about it all the time." She smiled. "And I am so thankful for it all. But I think I should at least have the interview."

Jack just sighed and waved goodbye to her as she exited his office. However, he was not about to give up. He immediately went on the offensive. He confided in Tess D'Emelia to write a heartfelt letter to Shelly, encouraging her to stay and move this agency onward and upward. He asked Meryl to suggest that she actually joined the small agency because of Shelly's belief and optimism about the place. He even asked his dad to write a note to her to suggest that she was "the best thing to happen to my son since your business union." As Jack told them all, lay on the guilt.

Then he called his law firm. The question was this: If we were to get bigger or be acquired by some advertising conglomerate, could I assign shares, basically "Even Steven," between Shelly and me? Perhaps forty-forty. With another twenty to be assigned to other key players?"

"That's easy," Robert Morgenthau, Esq., advised him. "Can I get something in writing by tomorrow afternoon?"

"That's a push," the lawyer advised, "but I can get you some document that might serve your needs."

Meanwhile, Jack sent the photo of the two of them from the *Adweek* article in front of the O'Brien, Lipschitz, and Partners logo, with the words "We belong together."

Later on, he sent another email to her. "Don't accept anything. Don't sign anything. We must talk."

The next morning, Shelly went to the BBDO office with her stackful of memos from her existing agency. On the elevator, she did have the heebie- jeebies and was even a little sick to her stomach. In the reception area, she reread the memos and was told by the receptionist that Mr. Bigwig was running about fifteen minutes late but was anxious to speak with her.

As she sat there, she again reviewed the emails from her cohorts and began to feel sicker to her stomach. After several minutes of self-reflection, staring at the ceiling, she approached the receptionist. "I think I may have a stomach virus," she explained. "I should reschedule. I'll call back for a new appointment."

The receptionist was most understanding. "Oh, I'm so sorry. Just call back when you feel better."

Shelly never did. Instead, she went back to O'Brien, Lipschitz, and Partners and walked into Jack O'Brien's office.

"What? They didn't come through on the money?" he asked sarcastically.

"They probably would," she explained. "But love beats money."

Instinctively, Jack pushed his chair back and walked toward his business partner. While he was never a very physical person, he did give her the biggest hug and told her that the very thought of continuing without her kept him up all night without sleep.

"I even thought of the new logo, 'O'Brien, O'Brien, and Partners,'" he said. "But despite the fact that I love my dad, it almost made me throw up. No, the name of this damn agency is O'Brien, Lipschitz, and Partners. And there is only one Lipschitz."

"Onward and upward," she said, as she did in the article.

That afternoon, he commissioned a photographer to take a picture of all employees in front of their logo. They were all holding hands with a slight jump in the air. It was ultimately published in *Adweek* as a thank-you for being named the best small agency of the year. The photos were distributed to every employee. Shelly Lipschitz, for one, put it in her forever scrapbook.

EPILOGUE
NOTHING LASTS FOREVER

Within the next six months, the agency actually accelerated. They won Schwinn Bicycles ("Ride for your life"), the Circle Line Tours ("Discover New York like a g.d. tourist"), and Run, Rock, Run (a political exploratory for the Rock, as he wondered whether or not he should be the next president). Within weeks, Jack revealed a legal document to Shelly that assured her that she would have 40 percent of the proceeds (exactly equal to his) if the agency were to go public or be bought out. He was quite proud of himself, and she was very appreciative that this proposition was not used as leverage in her negotiations with BBDO.

Despite Jack's hope that they would not get much bigger, they did. And they were eventually bought out by WPP. Both Shelly and Jack became millionaires. But neither one of them was as ever as happy as in the formative, experimental, and adventurous years at O'Brien, Lipschitz, and Partners.